A GHOSTLY HAUNTING
IN
GRAND HAVEN

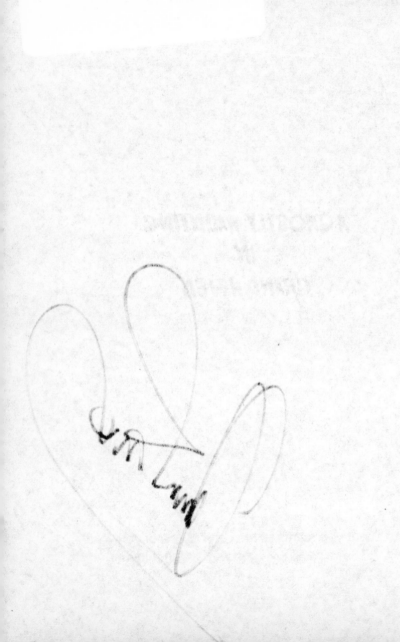

Here's what readers from around the country are saying about Johnathan Rand's AMERICAN CHILLERS:

"I have 23 of your books, but INCREDIBLE IVY OF IOWA is my very favorite. I've read it five times!"

-Conner P., age 11, Iowa

"Thanks for coming to our school! Everyone thought you were going to be really scary, but you were really funny. Come back next year!"

-Caroline M., 12, Arizona

"I get so freaked out when I read your books, but I can't stop!"

-Jack T., age 10, Florida

"Did all of these things that you write about really happen to you? My sister says they're all true stories, but she lies about everything."

-Thad A., Age 11, California

"MUTANT MAMMOTHS OF MONTANA was awesome! I'm from Montana, and that book was super-cool! Will you write another one about my state?"

-Shelley R., age 9, Montana

"I read about your camp at the back of one of your books, and I'm going to go when I get old enough. I love to write, and I can't wait!"

-Jordyn T., age 8, Illinois

"I have to tell you that you're my favorite author! I never liked reading before, until I read IDAHO ICE BEAST. I loved that book, and I even did a book report on it!"

-Mark R., age 10, Oregon

"Your dogs are so cute. Your books are good, but I like your dogs, too. You should write a book about them."

-Jasmine J., age 13, South Carolina

"I know you get a ton of mail, but I hope you read this. Everyone in my school is in love with your books! Our library has a bunch of them, but they're never on the shelves when I go to get another one."

-Preston N., age 9, Michigan

"We had a book fair at our school, and they had a bunch of your books. I bought three of them and I read all of them! They're great! I'm going to buy more when we have another book fair."

-Rachel S., age 11, Pennsylvania

"We took a vacation and went to Chillermania and you were there! Do you remember me? My name is Bryson, and I had blue shirt. I bought six books and a hat! My dad says we will come again next summer."

-Sam W., age 12, Tennessee

"Keep writing! I love all of your books, especially the Michigan Chillers, because that's where I'm from!"
-Aaron P., age 10, Michigan

"Thank you for writing me back! My friends didn't believe you would, but I showed them your letter and the bookmark you sent. That was so cool!"

-Kate B., age 10, Indiana

"My favorite book is SAVAGE DINOSAURS OF SOUTH DAKOTA. I think you should make movies out of all your books, especially this one!"

-Keith A., Age 11, New Jersey

"I started reading the Freddie Fernortner books, and now I'm reading all of your American Chillers books! I love all of them! I can't decide which one is my favorite."

-Jenna T., age 9, Minnesota

"After I read VIRTUAL VAMPIRES OF VERMONT, I had strange dreams. Does that happen to anyone else, or is it just me?"

-Anders B., age 12, Texas

"I read your books every night just before I go to bed. I have six of my own, but I borrow more from the library. I love all of them! Keep writing!"

-Annette O., age 11, Nebraska

Got something cool to say about Johnathan Rand's books? Let us know, and we might publish it right here! Send your short blurb to:

Chiller Blurbs
281 Cool Blurbs Ave.
Topinabee, MI 49791

Other books by Johnathan Rand:

Michigan Chillers:

#1: Mayhem on Mackinac Island
#2: Terror Stalks Traverse City
#3: Poltergeists of Petoskey
#4: Aliens Attack Alpena
#5: Gargoyles of Gaylord
#6: Strange Spirits of St. Ignace
#7: Kreepy Klowns of Kalamazoo
#8: Dinosaurs Destroy Detroit
#9: Sinister Spiders of Saginaw
#10: Mackinaw City Mummies
#11: Great Lakes Ghost Ship
#12: AuSable Alligators
#13: Gruesome Ghouls of Grand Rapids
#14: Bionic Bats of Bay City
#15: Calumet Copper Creatures
#16: Catastrophe in Caseville
#17: A Ghostly Haunting in Grand Haven

American Chillers:

#1: The Michigan Mega-Monsters
#2: Ogres of Ohio
#3: Florida Fog Phantoms
#4: New York Ninjas
#5: Terrible Tractors of Texas
#6: Invisible Iguanas of Illinois
#7: Wisconsin Werewolves
#8: Minnesota Mall Mannequins
#9: Iron Insects Invade Indiana
#10: Missouri Madhouse
#11: Poisonous Pythons Paralyze Pennsylvania
#12: Dangerous Dolls of Delaware
#13: Virtual Vampires of Vermont
#14: Creepy Condors of California
#15: Nebraska Nightcrawlers
#16: Alien Androids Assault Arizona
#17: South Carolina Sea Creatures
#18: Washington Wax Museum
#19: North Dakota Night Dragons
#20: Mutant Mammoths of Montana
#21: Terrifying Toys of Tennessee
#22: Nuclear Jellyfish of New Jersey
#23: Wicked Velociraptors of West Virginia
#24: Haunting in New Hampshire
#25: Mississippi Megalodon
#26: Oklahoma Outbreak
#27: Kentucky Komodo Dragons
#28: Curse of the Connecticut Coyotes

American Chillers (cont'd)

#31: The Nevada Nightmare Novel
#32: Idaho Ice Beast
#33: Monster Mosquitoes of Maine
#34: Savage Dinosaurs of South Dakota
#35: Maniac Martians Marooned in Massachusetts
#36: Carnivorous Crickets of Colorado
#37: The Underground Undead of Utah
#38: The Wicked Waterpark of Wyoming
#39: Angry Army Ants Ambush Alabama
#40: Incredible Ivy of Iowa
#41: North Carolina Night Creatures

Freddie Fernortner, Fearless First Grader:

#1: The Fantastic Flying Bicycle
#2: The Super-Scary Night Thingy
#3: A Haunting We Will Go
#4: Freddie's Dog Walking Service
#5: The Big Box Fort
#6: Mr. Chewy's Big Adventure
#7: The Magical Wading Pool
#8: Chipper's Crazy Carnival
#9: Attack of the Dust Bunnies from Outer Space!
#10: The Pond Monster
#11: Tadpole Trouble
#12: Frankenfreddie
#13: Day of the Dinosaurs

Adventure Club series:

#1: Ghost in the Graveyard
#2: Ghost in the Grand
#3: The Haunted Schoolhouse

For Teens:

PANDEMIA: A novel of the bird flu and the end of the world
(written with Christopher Knight)

American Chillers Double Thrillers:

Vampire Nation & Attack of the Monster Venus Melon

Johnathan Rand's
MICHIGAN
CHILLERS®

#17: A Ghostly Haunting
in
Grand Haven

Johnathan Rand

An AudioCraft Publishing, Inc. book

Book storage and warehouses provided by Chillermania!©
Indian River, Michigan

Michigan Chillers #17: A Ghostly Haunting in Grand Haven
ISBN 13-digit: 978-1-893699-02-1

Librarians/Media Specialists:
PCIP/MARC records available **free of charge** at
www.americanchillers.com

Cover illustration by Dwayne Harris
Cover layout and design by Sue Harring

Printed in USA

A GHOSTLY HAUNTING
IN
GRAND HAVEN

VISIT CHILLERMANIA!

WORLD HEADQUARTERS FOR BOOKS BY JOHNATHAN RAND!

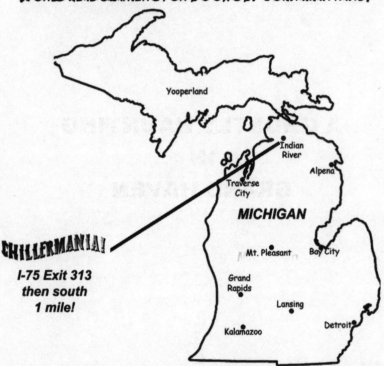

Yooperland

Indian River

Alpena

Traverse City

MICHIGAN

Mt. Pleasant

Bay City

CHILLERMANIA!

*I-75 Exit 313
then south
1 mile!*

Grand Rapids

Lansing

Detroit

Kalamazoo

Visit the HOME for books by Johnathan Rand! Featuring books, hats, shirts, bookmarks and other cool stuff not available anywhere else in the world! Plus, watch the American Chillers website for news of special events and signings at *CHILLERMANIA!* with author Johnathan Rand! Located in northern lower Michigan, on I-75! Take exit 313 . . . then south 1 mile! For more info, call (231) 238-0338. And be afraid! Be veeeery afraaaaaaiiiid . . . .

"Quinn, can you give me a hand for a minute?"

I rolled my eyes, closed my book, and put it on my bed. Whenever Dad asks me to help him out 'for a minute,' it's usually something that takes hours.

"Be right there," I called out. I sat up and got off my bed.

And I was just getting to a good part, I thought, glancing down at my book. Guess it'll have to wait.

I left my bedroom and walked down the hall

to the living room. Dad was kneeling in front of a gigantic steel contraption, a large, box-like piece of equipment with all sorts of switches, dials, blinking lights, meters, and a dark computer screen. Of course, this was nothing new. Dad was always working on electronic gadgetry, equipment that he designed and built himself.

Now, I'm sure lots of adults build electronic equipment as a hobby. But my dad is a little different. My dad is a ghost hunter. During the week, he works as a salesman at a car dealership. However, on the weekends, evenings, and almost every spare moment he has, he spends his time investigating haunted houses.

My friends think this is kind of cool, but in reality, I think my dad's a little nutty. I don't say that to be mean or disrespectful; I think even my dad himself knows he's a bit different. After all: how many parents will pick up their sons at school and then take them to what's reported to be a haunted house? My dad has done this with me dozens of times.

At first, I thought it was kind of fun. A few years ago, Dad was watching a ghost hunting show on television. He was completely fascinated, and by the time the show was over, he'd decided he wanted to be a ghost hunter, too. He read all sorts of books, watched all sorts of movies, and built his own equipment to try to detect ghosts. I went with him a bunch of times, but we never found any evidence of a real haunting. And we certainly didn't find any ghosts.

Still, my dad wasn't deterred. Once in a while, he would capture something on video, something that moved or didn't seem right, and he would claim that it was proof that it was a ghost. I didn't think so. I never saw anything—not a single thing—that led me to believe ghosts are real.

That was all about to change on a cold, snowy day in my own hometown of Grand Haven, Michigan.

2

Just as I suspected, I wound up helping Dad for a few hours. Something wasn't working right on the machine he'd been building, and I wound up handing him different tools while he tinkered away at the machine. Finally, later in the day, he got it working.

"There," he said proudly as he stood up. "Now, I'll be able to record variations of temperature to a digital file. The temperature

15

variations will be converted to a visible picture, and we'll be able to actually see the changes."

"Cool," I said, but I really wasn't all that interested. I was just glad the thing was fixed, so I could leave.

I went back to my bedroom and read for a while. Then, I put on my snowsuit, boots, hats, and gloves and went outside. It was snowing lightly, and across the street, Angela Parker was trying to build a snowman. Angela is my age—12—and I've known her all my life.

When she saw me, she smiled. She stopped what she was doing and waved with a gloved hand. I crossed the street.

"Trying to build a snowman?" I asked.

"It's not going very good," she said with a defeated shrug. "It's too cold, and the snow isn't packy."

"We're supposed to get a snowstorm tomorrow," I said, glancing up at the steely sky. "It's supposed to get a little warmer, and we're supposed to get a lot of heavy, wet snow."

"That'll be perfect for building snowmen," Angela said with a smart grin.

"And for having snowball fights," I said with an even wider smile.

Angela abandoned her attempts at making a snowman. Instead, we gathered up our sleds and hiked to a nearby hill. Although the conditions weren't very good for making snowmen, they were perfect for sledding. The snow was fast, and we spent the rest of the day speeding down the hill, flying over bumps and tumbling wildly off our sleds when we took a bad turn.

Later, when it started getting dark, we went to my house. Mom was home from work, and she offered to make us hot chocolate. Dad was still in the living room, fumbling around with his gigantic, electrical contraption.

"Is your dad still obsessed with hunting for ghosts?" Angela quietly asked me as she glanced at my dad in the living room.

I nodded and rolled my eyes. "He's bound and determined that he's going to find proof that ghosts exist."

"Maybe they do," Angela said.

"My dad is convinced that they're real," I said, "but in all the times I've ever been ghost hunting with him, I've never seen any proof. He seems to think that quick changes in temperature prove that ghosts exist. Or he'll see something that he thought moved on its own and think a ghost was responsible. But he's never been able to catch anything like that on camera. If you ask me, he's just wasting his time. Money, too. He's spent a lot of money on his ghost hunting hobby."

"What's that thing he's working on?" asked Angela.

"Some newfangled machine he designed and built on his own. He says the thing will actually be able to see changes in temperature when they happen. He says he'll be able to make a video that'll record the changes and convert them to computer images. You know, like real pictures of ghosts. He says that will be proof that a house really is haunted."

Angela sipped her hot chocolate. "If he actually can prove that ghosts exist," she said, "you guys will be rich."

"That would be nice," I said, shaking my head, "but I don't think it's going to happen."

Oh, it was going to happen, all right. Only, Dad wouldn't be the only one making the discovery. It was going to include Angela and me. For the first time in my life, I would have absolute, horrifying proof that ghosts are real, that haunted houses really do exist.

And it was all going to happen the very next day, in an old home on Lake Michigan, on the outskirts of Grand Haven.

3

The next day was Sunday. Dad made eggs and bacon, as he always does on Sunday mornings. My older brother, Alex, slept in and missed breakfast. So, it was just Mom, Dad, and me sitting around the table.

"A big snowstorm is supposed to move in later today," Mom said.

"Cool," I said. "I hope we get so much snow that they close school tomorrow."

"I'm going to need your help again today," Dad said, and he popped a piece of bacon into his mouth. "There's a house over on North Shore Drive, on Lake Michigan. Tony isn't going to be able to make it today, and I'm going to need some help with my equipment."

Tony Simms is a friend of my dad's. They often hunt ghosts together. Sometimes, I think Mr. Simms is nuttier than my dad.

I really didn't want to help, but I didn't see any way to get out of it. Besides: it probably wouldn't take too long.

"Do I have to stay?" I asked.

Dad shook his head. "It'll only be for a couple of hours, and all I need is for you to help me load the gear into the house. There's a big hill in front of it, on the lake side, and you can bring your sled if you want."

That sounded fun. While it would be kind of boring to hang out inside the house while my dad fiddled around with equipment, it would be a blast to find a new sledding hill.

"Can Angela come?" I asked.

Dad shrugged. "Sure, if she wants to."

I called Angela after breakfast and asked if she wanted to come along.

"Is it a haunted house?" she asked.

"My dad probably thinks so, or else he wouldn't be hauling all of his equipment over there."

"Sure, I'll go," Angela replied. "That sounds like a lot of fun. Sledding, that is."

"Good," I said. "Come on over any time."

Angela knocked on the door about ten minutes later, wearing her red winter coat, black snow pants, black boots, a red hat, and red mittens. We helped Dad break down all of his equipment in his garage workshop and load it into the back of his van. Then, we climbed inside and were on our way.

The sky was gray, and it was snowing lightly. Tree limbs reached into the sky with their wiry, bony fingers. An inch of new snow covered the ground and roads. Again, I found myself hoping that there wouldn't be school the next day. That would mean an extra day of sledding and playing outside.

It was going to take us only twenty minutes to get to the house. While he drove, Dad told us a little bit about the old home.

"A retired couple recently bought the house and moved in," he explained. "Soon after, strange things started happening. Things started moving on their own, and the man and woman started hearing weird noises and even voices. One night, they even saw a ghostly figure walking down the stairs. It scared them so much that they decided to move to a hotel while they figured out what to do. They haven't returned to the house since."

"So they called you?" I asked.

"Yep," Dad replied with a nod. "They want to find out for sure if the place really is haunted."

"Then, what are they going to do?" Angela asked. "I mean, if it's really haunted, what happens then?"

"I don't know," said Dad. "I don't get rid of

ghosts; I just find them."

I looked at Angela, and she grinned and rolled her eyes. I knew she was thinking the same thing I was: Dad had never found any proof that ghosts are real.

We turned right onto North Shore Drive and headed north. After going about a half mile, Dad slowed the van.

"There's the driveway, up ahead," he said, pointing.

Dad turned left, and we went down a winding driveway lined with snow on each side. By now, the snow was really coming down. Big, fluffy flakes the size of cotton balls created a curtain of white in front of the van. It was snowing so hard that it was difficult to see much of the driveway.

"Looks like you might get your wish," Dad said.

"What's that?" I asked.

"If it keeps snowing like this," Dad said with a casual wave of his hand, "you're not going to have school tomorrow."

"I hope so," I said.

"Me, too," said Angela. "We haven't had a snow day in a long time."

The snow was falling so hard that it obscured the view of the house. We didn't see it until we were right in front of it, and let me tell you: I got a sudden chill that had nothing to do with the cold weather or the snow.

But it was Angela who suddenly gasped and pointed. Her eyes bulged.

"Oh, my gosh!" she said. "Look at that!"

At first, I didn't see anything.

"What?" I asked. "What is it?"

"Right there!" Angela said excitedly. "Standing next to that tree!"

I strained my eyes to see through the falling snow.

"I see it!" Dad said.

Finally, I could make out the dark figure. It was a white-tailed deer! Which, of course, wasn't all that uncommon. We often saw deer near our home and, actually, all over Michigan. However, we were really close to her. In fact, I don't think I'd ever been so close to a deer before.

Quick as a flash, the deer bounded off into the nearby woods, where she vanished.

"That was cool!" Angela said. "She was really close."

Then, our attention returned to the old house. Through the thick haze of heavily falling snow, we could make out its features. It was three stories tall, with lots of windows. A couple of rooms on the upper floors had sliding glass doors with balconies. I assumed they must be bedrooms or rooms for entertaining.

And it was Angela who said the exact same thing I had been thinking.

"This place is creepy," she said. "Who on Earth would want to live in a place like this?"

"Actually," Dad said, "there's a lot of history behind this house. It was built in the 1920s and was owned by some famous movie star. Not sure who. But there have been reports of the house being haunted going all the way back to the time it was built."

While I didn't believe in ghosts, I had to admit that if there ever was such a thing as a haunted house, I was looking at it. Angela was right: it definitely was creepy-looking.

"Well, let's go have a look," Dad said. "Then, we'll move all of my gear inside."

Angela and I slipped out the passenger side door, and Dad exited the driver's side. The three of us walked through the falling snow to the house, where we stopped at the front porch. Dad dug a single key from his jacket pocket.

"Here we go," he said, and he stepped onto the porch, slid the key into the lock, and pushed the front door open. "Don't forget to knock the snow off your boots."

Dad stepped into the house, and Angela and I followed.

We were in a large foyer with eggshell-colored walls. There was a wooden coat rack with several coats hanging on it. A few pairs of shoes and boots were placed next to the wall, and there was a closet with the door hanging open a few inches. It was filled with various winter coats.

Dad continued walking, and we followed him down a carpeted hallway lined with colorful paintings on the walls. We came to a kitchen on our left, and to our right was an enormous living room with a huge fireplace made of large, rounded stones. The room was filled with furniture, and there were many pictures and paintings on the walls. There was an empty coffee mug on a small table in front of the couch. A book was upside down and open on the armrest of a lounge chair. A pair of slippers were placed next to the fireplace.

"It looks like they just got up and left everything," Angela said.

"I think that's what they did," Dad said. "The man told me that he and his wife were so frightened that they didn't take time to pack anything more than a suitcase full of clothing. They wanted out of the house, and fast."

Now that I was in the house, I didn't have that creepy feeling that I had before. Outside, when I was looking at it through the falling snow, there was something strange, something unnerving about the home. Inside, it didn't appear to be anything more than it was: an old home built a long time ago.

Dad walked into the kitchen. When he was out of hearing range, I turned to Angela and smiled.

"See any ghosts?"

Angela shook her head and smiled. "Not a single one," she replied. "I'm more interested in finding that sledding hill."

On the far side of the living room was a big picture window that faced Lake Michigan. We walked to it, but it was snowing so hard that the only thing we could see was a wall of white and our own blurry reflections in the glass. We could hear the wind gusting against the house, blowing snow up and around the eaves.

"That hill could be right there," I said, tapping the glass. "But it's snowing so hard that we would never be able to see it."

Dad called out from the kitchen. "Okay,

guys," he said, "let's get that stuff hauled in, so I can get started."

He was already in the hallway, and Angela and I followed him back into the foyer. That was where we found something very strange.

Strange . . . but not scary or horrifying.

No, the scary, horrifying things were to come later. But what we were about to discover in the foyer should have given us a warning that someone—or something—was in the house besides us.

Dad was already through the front door and on the porch when Angela stopped in the foyer and stared at the closet. I was behind her, so I stopped, too.

"What's wrong?" I asked.

She gestured with her right arm, pointing with her red mitten. "The closet door," she said. She had a puzzled look on her face.

I looked at the closet. "What about it?"

"It was open a little bit when we came in

here. Now, it's closed."

I looked at the closed closet door. Although I was warmly dressed from head to toe, that didn't stop an odd chill from forming at the base of my neck and trickling down my spine. But as I looked through the open front door, at the snow swirling around the porch, at the figure of my dad as he trudged back to our van, the chill in my back faded. My uneasiness subsided.

"The front door was open while we were in the living room," I said. "The wind must've blown the closet door closed."

"Yeah," Angela agreed. "You're probably right." A playful grin bloomed on her face. "Come on. Let's get your dad's stuff loaded into the house. Then, we can go sledding!"

It didn't take us long to finish dragging Dad's gear into the house. One of the machines was heavy, and it took all three of us to carry it inside. Dad stumbled on the porch and nearly fell, but he was able to recover. Good thing, too. Not only could he have twisted an ankle, but if we had dropped the heavy machine we were carrying, all three of us could have been hurt.

All the while, Dad jabbered on and on and on. We just listened to him, but once in a while, I would mutter "hmmm" or "uh-huh" to let him know I was paying attention, even though I really wasn't. I'd heard all of Dad's ghost hunting talk before.

"But this time," Dad said as if reading my mind, "this time, things are going to be different. If this place really is haunted, I'm going to get actual video footage. It's the proof we need to show the world that ghosts really do exist."

"That'll be great," I said, trying the best I could to sound interested as we carried the last of the gear inside.

When we had finally finished unloading, Angela and I retrieved our plastic sleds from the van. As it turned out, the hill wasn't far away at all. It was on the other side of the thick clump of trees and sloped down toward the lake. And it was steep, too! Angela and I had a great time speeding down the hill on our sleds and then racing up to do it again.

Finally, after a couple of hours, we grew tired of walking back up the hill and decided to go back to the house. By now, the snow was coming down heavier than ever, and the wind had increased. It was looking more and more like school would be canceled the next day. Hot dog.

As we approached the house, Angela stopped. She stared.

"What?" I asked.

"I don't know," she replied. "I guess with the blowing snow and the wind, the house looks kind of creepy. I mean . . . more creepy than before."

I looked at the house and then at our van parked in the driveway. The wind howled; the snow sailed. Angela was right: it really did look kind of creepy in the gusting snowstorm.

"Come on," I said, shrugging it off. "It's too bad we don't have any hot chocolate to warm us up."

We trudged toward the house, dragging our sleds, unaware that our horrifying ordeal was about to begin.

Inside the house, there was no sign of Dad.

"Hey, Dad!" I shouted. "Where did you go?"

At first, I wasn't alarmed. But when we didn't find him in the living room, and when he didn't return my repeated yells, a small rock settled in my stomach.

"He's got to be around here somewhere," Angela said. "I mean, he couldn't just disappear."

We were standing next to his homemade

machine in the living room. The apparatus looked like a washer and dryer, one on top of the other, with a computer monitor on top. There were a few other metal component boxes lit with flashing lights, humming with electricity, making strange sounds. Cables coiled and snaked around and onto the floor. On the computer screen, we could see the live video footage of the living room. Dad had positioned a camera on a tripod next to his giant machine.

"Dad?" I called out again, a little louder this time. My voice was filled with concern, and maybe even a little panic. I was beginning to get worried.

Angela took off her red mittens, dropped them on a chair, and pointed at the computer screen.

"We're looking at live footage right now," she said. "Is there any way we can play it back?"

While I wasn't familiar with Dad's machine, I knew my way around computers and electronic gizmos pretty well. I took off my gloves and, with my bare fingers, began fiddling with the keyboard. The screen went dark.

"What happened?" Angela asked.

"I returned the file to its very beginning," I replied. "Let's play some of it back."

On the computer screen, the living room suddenly came into view. It looked the same as it had before, but I knew that we were looking into the past, at a recorded video. I found the fast-forward function on the software program and pressed it.

At first, it didn't look like anything had changed. Then, Dad came into view on the screen, walking through the living room. However, because we had the file on fast-forward, Dad was moving in high speed. He looked kind of funny, like some of those old Keystone Cops movies that I had seen, the ones with that funny piano music. His movements were jerky and quick, cartoon-like. Angela and I laughed out loud.

Then, the same familiar scene returned, and the screen showed just the living room with all of the stuff the owners left behind and the pictures on the walls.

Suddenly, something else began to appear

on the computer screen.

"Wait a minute," Angela said in a tense whisper. Her arm shot out, and she pointed at the screen. "What ... What on Earth is that?!?!"

An image was forming on the computer screen, something in the middle of the living room. It began as a fuzzy white ball and continued to grow. I tapped the computer keyboard and slowed the file down to normal speed. Angela and I watched, both amazed and horrified, as the entity began to grow and grow on the computer screen.

Soon, it was unmistakable. Arms, legs. A head. The body was motionless, for the most part, but appeared to waver slowly back and forth, gently, as if in a breeze. Still, there was no doubt what we were seeing.

"Oh, my gosh," Angela whispered. "I can't... I can't believe we're seeing this."

My world was crashing down, shaken by this new information. The rock in my stomach had grown to the size of a boulder, heavy and solid, knotted and tight.

I had always thought my dad was a little off

his rocker for believing in hauntings and other weird, supernatural things. After all, I hadn't seen any evidence that proved ghosts existed—

Until now.

We watched for what seemed like hours, but, in reality, was only about a minute. On the screen before us, nothing had changed. The ghostly image remained, although it was unclear whether it was a man or a woman. It was definitely a human shape, but it wasn't clear enough to tell anything more. I couldn't make out any facial or body features other than arms, legs, a torso, and a head.

Then, we saw another movement. Dad came

into the picture! He was moving very slowly, cautiously, toward the entity floating in the middle of the living room. It was obvious that he had spotted the thing on the computer screen and was approaching it.

I shot a nervous glance around the room, wondering if this entity, whatever it was, was watching us at this very moment. I saw nothing except the furnishings, the walls, the ceiling, and the blowing snow whipping outside the window. The wind howled, and it gave me a lonely, desolate feeling. I didn't like the fact that we were all alone in the house. Sure, Dad was somewhere, but we didn't know where. For the time being, it was just Angela and me.

While we watched the screen, we saw my dad cautiously approach the misty-white figure. Slowly, he reached out to the apparition, waving his hands back and forth in a sweeping motion. From what we could see on the computer screen, it looked as if his hand was moving right through the entity!

We continued to watch, fascinated by the

scene on the screen in front of us. Dad waved his arms back and forth a few more times, but they went right through the ghost, as easily as a hand slicing through smoke.

"This is unbelievable," Angela said quietly.

Then, the ghost began to shimmer. It drifted back a couple of feet and then moved off to the left of the screen. Dad stood motionless for a moment . . . and then he began to follow. His steps were cautious and wary, and his eyes never left the entity. The ghost vanished to the left of the screen, leaving the living room. Dad followed, and he, too, vanished from the screen. Then, we were staring at nothing but the screen showing the living room interior.

"Where did they go?" I asked.

Angela shrugged. "Over there, somewhere," she replied, pointing to the hall that led to the front door. "The ghost went down the hallway, and your dad followed."

"Let's go that way, then," I said.

"Are you nuts?" Angela asked.

"Come on, Angela," I said. "We just came

that way, anyway. We were just outside and walked down the hall to get here. Nothing happened to us. Besides: we've got to find out where Dad is."

Without another word, we wound around the large machine, through the living room, and into the hall. Like Dad had done, we took slow, cautious steps. I kept turning my head from side to side, expecting at any moment to see some sort of haunting apparition, some sort of ghost staring back at me. I saw nothing.

We reached the foyer. We'd left the front door open and snow had blown in, and there was a dusty covering of white near the door. I grabbed the knob and pushed the door closed.

"So," Angela said, "where did they go?"

"They had to come this way," I replied. "We saw them on the computer screen."

"But they're not here," Angela said. "If they came this way, they had to leave through the front door. You and I just came through here a few minutes ago, and we didn't see anything."

I took a step forward and opened the front

door. The snowstorm had grown to monstrous proportions, like a white witch who screamed and shrieked and raged. Large flakes of snow billowed and swirled in whirling hurricane patterns.

Angela pointed to the porch. "See?" she said. "Those are our tracks, right there. There aren't any more tracks. If your dad came this way, he would've made tracks in the snow."

I closed the front door, and Angela and I looked around the foyer.

"This is crazy," I said. "Where did Dad go?"

The answer, as we were about to find out, was more shocking than we could have ever imagined.

I scratched my head.

"This doesn't make any sense," I said. "My dad couldn't just vanish into thin air."

"Maybe he's still in the house somewhere," Angela said.

"Dad?" I called out again. "Dad? Can you hear me?"

There was no answer. The only sound we heard was the crazed, white witch howling outside, casting her ferocious wintry spell.

"He's got to be here, somewhere inside the house," I said. "Come on. Let's find him."

Cautiously, Angela and I left the foyer, walked through the hallway, and turned left into the kitchen. The light was on, and we could see our reflections in the large windows that faced the lake. It had grown dark outside, so we couldn't see anything beyond the glass. Not even the snow.

"I'm not so sure this is a good idea," Angela said. I noticed that she was walking closely, afraid to get too far away. She was scared, and I couldn't blame her. Something really strange was going on, and until we found out what happened to Dad, I wasn't going to relax. Neither was Angela.

"We'll be fine," I said. "Dad has to be around here somewhere."

"Yeah," Angela replied, "but you're forgetting one thing. If your Dad is around here, that ghost is, too."

This was something that had been rattling around in the back of my mind, but I didn't want to think about it. On the computer screen, the ghost had simply appeared from nowhere. It was terrifying to think that at any moment, it could materialize in front of us!

Absently, I walked over to the counter and opened up a drawer. Inside, I found a bunch of utensils, including steel knives, forks, and spoons. I picked up one of the knives, thinking that I could use it as a weapon. Then, I returned it to the drawer. After all: what good is a knife going to do against a ghost? We had watched Dad's hands go right through the white apparition in the living room. A knife would have the same effect, making it worthless.

And besides: something told me that if the ghost wanted to harm us, he was going to do it, whether we liked it or not. There was nothing we would be able to do about it.

I opened another drawer. It was filled with odds and ends and all sorts of things.

A junk drawer, I thought. We have one of these at our house. A drawer in the kitchen that's filled with all kinds of things that don't have any particular home. Everybody has a junk drawer in their house.

I pawed through some of the items and found a flashlight about the size of the palm of my hand. I clicked it on, and a dull splotch of light appeared on the wall. Thinking that it might come in handy, I held it up and turned to Angela.

"Look what I—"

I stopped speaking. Angela was gone.

"Angela?" I said. "Where did you go?"

"I'm here, in the foyer!" she called back, her voice filled with urgency and surprise. "Come here, quick! You're not going to believe what I found in the closet!"

I stuffed the flashlight in my coat pocket, hurried through the kitchen, bounded down the hallway, and found Angela in the foyer. She was standing in front of the closet, a pile of coats on the floor at her feet. The closet door was open, and she was pointing inside.

"Look!" she said. Her eyes were wide and filled with disbelief. "Look what I found!"

I took a step closer and looked into the

closet, where she was pointing.

I froze.

"No way!" I said.

It was a hidden staircase!

The coats had covered it up, and we hadn't seen it before. Now that Angela had moved them out of the way, we could clearly see wooden steps descending into darkness.

"Why would someone put a staircase in a closet?" I wondered aloud.

"Because they wanted to hide it," Angela replied. "For whatever reason, nobody is supposed to find this."

Remembering the flashlight, I dug it out of my pocket and turned it on. Unfortunately, it wasn't strong enough to illuminate much, and the darkness in the stairway swallowed the light.

"I wonder what's down there," Angela replied.

"I'll bet that's where Dad went," I said.

"But there aren't any lights on," Angela replied. "He'd fall and break his neck."

"My dad doesn't always think about things

like that," I replied. I didn't mean it as an insult to my dad, but sometimes, he did things without thinking about them. Even my mom would agree with that.

"Dad?" I called down the staircase. "Dad? Are you down there? Can you hear me?"

No reply.

Outside, the old, winter witch continued to rage. Her wind was frantic and feverish, screaming at the windows, howling around the eaves and front door. Occasionally, the house made tired creaks and groans. It was eerie, and it made things seem even scarier than they probably were.

I took a single step over the coats and placed my foot on the first stair. Then, I turned to Angela.

"Are you coming?" I asked.

"I'm not going to let you go alone," she replied. "Besides," she said, looking around. "I don't think I want to be by myself in this house anymore. We're better off sticking together."

"Stay close behind me, watch your step, and don't fall."

Although the flashlight beam wasn't very

bright, it illuminated the steps in front of my feet. The wood was old and weathered, and it creaked as I took another step. Slowly, ever so slowly, step-by-step, Angela and I descended down the stairs. Slowly, cautiously, we made our way guided by the faint beam. Farther and farther we went, down, down, until it felt like we had been swallowed alive by the darkness.

10

The darkness was cold and lonely and needy. It seemed alive. Even with the dim flashlight, it was as if we were descending into the gullet of the house, burrowing into its bottomless belly. The steps creaked beneath our feet, and the deeper we descended, the less we could hear the howling wind outside.

Finally, we reached the bottom of the stairs. Here, the silence was maddening. We could no longer hear the wind at all. There were no creaks, no groans or moans from the house. Just—

Silence.

"This is really, really creepy," Angela whispered. She was standing so close behind me that I could feel her breath on my neck.

"Dad?" I called out. My voice faded quickly. There was no echo. "Dad? Are you down here? Can you hear me?"

I shined the weak flashlight beam in front of us. The light was faint and watery, and we couldn't see much: some shelves, what appeared to be some crates or boxes, and one very large box near a far wall to the right of us.

"It doesn't look like there's anything here," Angela replied. "I mean, it just looks like a normal basement."

I shined the beam around, trying to find a light switch on a wall or maybe a single pullstring hanging down. There was nothing. And when I shined the beam on the ceiling, sweeping it back and forth, I didn't even see any light bulbs.

"What was that over there?" Angela asked.

"Over to the right, by the wall?"

I shined the light in the direction she had indicated. About twenty feet away was a large box. It was rectangular in shape, probably six feet long, and was laying sideways on the floor. It look like it was a refrigerator laying on its side, only not quite as big.

Slowly, I approached it. Angela grabbed my arm and followed.

"It's just some sort of big wooden box," I said. "It's probably used for storage."

"See what's inside," Angela urged.

I wasn't sure if it was a good idea. It didn't really matter what was inside. We were looking for Dad, and I was certain that he wouldn't be hiding inside a box. Dad can sometimes be a practical joker and would do things to scare me and my brother, but he wouldn't take things this far.

Still, like Angela, I was curious.

"It's probably just tools and stuff," I replied.

Holding the flashlight with my right hand, I knelt down and felt around the top of the wooden box. My fingers caught an edge, and I lifted. The lid was heavy, but it moved smoothly, opening on hinges like a book.

I shined the light inside.

Angela drew a thick, deep breath. She held it, and I could feel her hands tighten around my right arm, gripping me so tightly that I nearly dropped the flashlight. I could only stare at the contents of the box.

No, not a box, I thought.

A black flower of grim horror began to bloom slowly in my gut, its icy petals worming through my body, wrapping around my muscles and tightening around my heart and squeezing my chest and darkening my mind. I felt dizzy.

It's not a box at all. It's a coffin. It's a coffin, and that's a skeleton . . . .

11

Angela's body trembled, and one hand flew to her mouth to stifle a scream. Her grip on my arm was now so strong that I was sure it was going to cut off my circulation. Her hold on my arm caused me to grip the flashlight even harder.

But I couldn't take my eyes away from the gray, bare bones laying in the coffin. They held me in a trance, captivated by some sinister spell, and I couldn't look away. I knew Angela was caught by the same dark mystery, and our eyes remained transfixed, focused on the gruesome contents of the coffin.

"Is . . . is that . . . is that what I think it is?" Angela stammered.

"I think so," I said quietly.

"We have to get out of here," she said. "We have to get out of here now." She was speaking in a whisper, but she was insistent. She sounded scared. Scared, and worried.

Still, neither of us could take our eyes from the grotesque scene before us.

"Let go of my arm," I said. "You're going to break it in half."

Angela released her grip, and I relaxed my arm and my hold of the flashlight. Slowly, I swept the beam up and down, long ways, beginning at the skeleton's feet and moving up to its skull. As the beam traveled upward, the bones created a forest of moving shadows on the inside wall of the coffin.

"Let's go," Angela whispered, louder this time, more insistently.

"Okay," I said, and I slowly lowered the coffin lid. At the same time, I noticed that the flashlight beam was rapidly dimming. There was no telling how old the batteries were or how much they'd been used. But by the looks of it, they weren't going to last much longer.

And that would mean we'd no longer have light. We wouldn't be able to see.

A faint noise came from Angela's stomach, sort of a low, long moan. At least, I thought it came from Angela's stomach.

"Was that . . . was that you?" she asked. "Did you make that sound?"

"I thought it was your stomach," I replied. I shined the faint beam of light in her face, and she squinted and shook her head. Then, I swept the flashlight around the room.

The sound came again, louder, and now I was certain that it hadn't come from Angela's stomach. But it seemed to be echoing, drifting, as if it came from all around us, in every direction. A long, mournful sound, the sound of someone groaning in pain.

"Let's go back upstairs," I said. "The batteries in the flashlight are almost dead."

I swept the weak beam around as we turned and began to hustle back through the basement. All around us, the eerie moan rose and fell like the wind: strong, then faint, stronger again, then softer . . . .

I stopped suddenly, realizing that something was really, really wrong. Besides the skeleton, besides the moaning and groaning in our ears. Besides my missing Dad.

I swept the flashlight beam around, and the yellow circle splatted on the floor and crept up the wall.

Something is really, really wrong . . . .

"Where . . . where are the steps?" Angela asked. "Where is the stairway that leads in and out of the basement?"

Where it should have been, it wasn't. Where we should have seen it, we didn't.

The staircase had vanished, leaving us in the basement by ourselves . . . with no way out.

12

My heart was already firing like a machine gun in my chest, but a sudden wave of heat surged through my bloodstream as another blast of panic electrified my veins. Faint as it was, I swept the flashlight beam about in a frenzy, unable to believe that the staircase had simply vanished.

But it was true.

I spun around, bouncing the beam up and down around the room until I'd made a complete circle. All the while, the ghostly moaning and groaning continued. Angela remained behind me, her hands on my shoulders, turning with me.

"It's gone," I whispered. "I know it's not possible, but it's not here anymore."

"I wish I'd never come here with you," Angela said with a sniffle. "I wish I was at home, watching television or playing video games or sledding. I wish I wasn't here."

"I didn't have any idea about this house," I pleaded. It had sounded as though Angela was blaming me for our troubles. "If I would have known these things were going to happen, I wouldn't have come in the first place."

"I . . . I didn't mean that it was your fault," Angela replied. "I'm sorry. I just . . . I just wish we were somewhere else."

I did, too.

"Well, wishing isn't going to get us out of here," I said, trying to sound brave and in-command. "We have to do something. We have to find a way out of here."

The ghostly moaning continued.

The flashlight dimmed.

"But how?" Angela said. "We're in a basement. If it's like the basement of our house, there's only one way in and one way out."

Angela was right. Most basements, including ours, had only one set of steps leading up and down. Some homes had windows in their basements, but those were positioned high on the wall and level with the ground outside. This basement had no windows and, apparently, no other entrance or exit.

The flashlight batteries finally gave out, and the glowing beam coughed, gasped, and died. Almost immediately, the eerie moaning and groaning around us faded, faded, faded more, and then it was gone. We heard nothing, no sounds at all. Not even the raging wind outside. The sounds of the moaning and groaning had been bad enough, but the pristine silence was just as sinister, just as creepy.

In the darkness, I felt for Angela's hand, gave it a squeeze, and held it.

"Don't worry," I said. "We'll find a way out.

There's got to be a way."

I think I sounded pretty confident, but I wasn't all that sure myself. Still, I tried to keep telling myself there was some reasonable explanation for what was happening. As bizarre as it was, I still wanted to believe that there were no such things as ghosts. I wanted to believe that things don't simply appear on a computer screen. I wanted to believe that staircases don't vanish.

And I really wanted to believe that my dad didn't vanish, either.

In fact, even after everything we'd experienced, I'd nearly convinced myself that there was some sort of explanation for everything. Maybe this was all some big joke, a prank that someone was playing on all three of us.

And that's what I was thinking, standing in the dark basement with Angela, when murky, gray forms began to appear all around us . . . .

13

Angela noticed the strange figures appearing at the exact moment I did. I was still holding her hand, and I could feel her cringe and draw closer, huddling next to me.

"What's going on?!?!" she hissed into my shoulder.

I had no answer, so I didn't say anything.

All around us, clouds of smoke began to form. At least, that's what they looked like: puffs of large, gray, blob-like entities that had no real shape or form to them.

But very soon, they began to morph into figures.

Human figures.

They were faint and hard to make out, but we could see arms and legs and torsos and heads. I counted five 'people' in all . . . if you could call them 'people.' They seemed to drift and float in the darkness, moving about without the use of their legs. It was as if they were on wheels connected to a rope, being pulled around us by some unseen person.

And as their features became clearer, we could make out the faint characteristics of their faces: their noses, lips, chins, and cheeks. There were three men and two women, although we couldn't really tell what they were wearing. I mean, it looked like the men were wearing nice suit coats and the women were wearing dresses, but other than that, their appearance below their necks was too murky and undefined.

Despite the cold terror I felt, the chill of

horror racing through my veins, I managed to speak.

"My dad's right," I muttered quietly.

"Huh?" Angela said.

"My dad's right," I repeated, this time in a louder whisper. "I've been making fun of him all this time, because I didn't believe in ghosts. He was right all along. Ghosts really are real. They really do exist."

"But who are they?" Angela croaked.

I shook my head slowly. It was a question I couldn't answer.

It was pointless to try to do anything. The flashlight had died, and we couldn't see a thing besides the ghostly figures. And the staircase, as crazy as it sounded, had vanished. I had no idea how we were going to get out of the basement.

So, we just watched. We watched, our bodies trembling, as the five phantom figures moved around us. Perhaps strangest of all was the fact that the ghosts didn't look at us. If they knew we were there, they gave no indication. Their eyes seemed to gaze off into the distance, and even when it appeared as though they were looking at us, their gaze was vacant and unseeing.

Dead.

Well, I thought, that would only make sense. After all, ghosts are, in fact, dead.

Then, as if things hadn't already been strange enough, the five figures began to vanish. Just as they had appeared, the three men and two women shimmered and shook and took on a loose, smoke-like appearance. They swirled slowly, their luminosity fading, becoming thinner and thinner, fainter and fainter. As the foggy figures vanished, a welcome wave of relief washed over me. Finally, when they were completely gone, a heavy sigh exploded from my mouth. I hadn't realized it, but I'd been holding my breath the entire time.

"I want to go home," Angela whimpered.

"I do, too," I said. And although I was feeling a moment of dark despair, I gathered up all my courage and decided that we would, in fact, get out. At least, that's what I told myself. It didn't matter that I really didn't believe it. I knew that if I said it to myself over and over, I'd begin to believe it. And like my mom says: before you do anything, you have to already believe that you can do it.

"Don't worry," I told Angela. "There's a way out of here, and we're going to find it. We're going to find my dad. We're going to be okay."

Then, I gave her hand a squeeze. Very cautiously, I took a step forward, tugging Angela along through the forbidding darkness without a clue where we were going . . . or what we were about to discover.

"Where are we going?" Angela asked.

"There has to be a way out of here," I said confidently, "and we're going to find it."

At least, I hoped we would find it. And I hoped that my voice didn't betray the fear that was gnawing at my flesh, eating away just beneath my skin. Because the truth was that I was scared. Really scared. But I didn't want Angela to know it.

"So, your dad is right, after all," Angela said

quietly.

"Yeah, he is," I replied. "I feel sorta bad, because I always thought he was kind of kooky. But now that we've seen the proof ourselves, I guess he was right all along. How about you? Did you ever believe that ghosts were real?"

"I guess I did when I was little," Angela replied. "And I think I've always known that there are some strange things in the world. Things that we don't understand. But as I got older, I guess I just began to think that ghosts were just make-believe."

"Me, too," I replied. "But just because you don't understand something doesn't mean it doesn't exist."

"You're right," Angela said. "I mean . . . I don't understand what's going on with this house. But whatever it is, it's really, really weird. And scary."

I was taking short, slow steps in the inky darkness, waving my right hand in front of me, trying to find a wall, trying to find anything. I knew that it was probably pointless and hopeless, but it was better than just standing there in the dark, doing nothing.

"I hope we don't bump into that coffin," Angela said.

Just as she said those words, my hand brushed something. I stopped walking and felt around with my hand.

"I think I found a wall," I said.

"Yay," Angela said. "That means we're safe."

I could tell that she was just being sarcastic, and I had to smile. Despite the fact that we were both terrified, she still had a small sense of humor.

I let go of her hand.

"Stay close," I said, and I felt the cool wall with my other hand, taking one more small step and pressing myself closer. In my mind, I was trying to remember everything I could about the basement, but there wasn't much. After all: the only things we'd seen were what we'd been able to spot in the dying beam of the flashlight.

The wall was cold and rough beneath my fingers, and I recognized it instantly as cement bricks. I felt around with both hands, but found nothing else but the solid wall.

Blindly, slowly, I reached back with my left hand.

"Ow!" Angela said. "You poked me in the eye."

"Sorry 'bout that," I replied. "I was trying to poke your ear. Grab my hand. I found the wall."

In the darkness, Angela's hand found mine. Cautiously, I led the way, following the wall with my right hand, feeling the cool brick beneath my fingers. The only sound was the slight scuffing of our boots and the gentle swishing of our winter clothing.

"All right, wait a minute," I said. "I found a corner."

We stopped. The corner I'd discovered wasn't a corner of the room, but a sharp edge of the wall. The brick. Moving my hand more, I discovered that there was a turn, as if we'd found a hallway that went off to the right.

"What did you find?" Angela asked.

"I'm not sure," I said, waving my right hand around in the darkness before me. "But I think I found a hallway."

By continuing to slowly wave my arm around, I soon discovered that not only had we come to a hallway that led off to the right, but there was also a narrow passageway that continued on directly ahead of us. I tried to get a picture in my mind of the layout of the basement and where we were in relation to the house above us.

"Okay," I said. "There's a hall that leads straight ahead and another one that goes off to the right."

"Which way do we go?" Angela asked.

"I'm not sure," I said. "But my guess would be that the hallway to the right would take us farther under the house. The one that leads ahead of us, straight, would take us farther away, out into the yard."

"So, let's go to the right and see if it's a way out of here."

I was just about to suggest that, but Angela had been thinking the same thing: maybe, just maybe, the hallway was a way out.

"Okay," I said, "to the right it is. Come on."

We started out again, and my mind whirled with questions. I was confused, worried, anxious, and nervous. But mostly, I was scared, and I'm not ashamed to admit it. I was afraid of what we'd already experienced; I was afraid that I might never see my dad again. I was afraid that we'd never get out of the house. And I was afraid that, at any moment, those weird, ghostly apparitions would appear. Sure, they hadn't hurt us or anything, but that didn't matter.

Maybe that's what scared me the most: the unknown. Not knowing what was going to happen next, not knowing if we were going to be okay. Not knowing if we were going to make it out of the house alive. Not knowing if—

And that's what I was thinking when my foot smacked into something solid, filling me with alarm and causing me to stop walking . . . .

15

"What is it?"

Angela spoke as soon as she heard the thud of my boot hitting something. We stopped walking, and I let go of her hand.

"I don't know," I said, but as I knelt down and reached out, I immediately had my answer. "Steps!" I said. "It's another stairway!"

"Let's hope it leads out of here," said Angela.

"Let's hope it doesn't vanish, too," I said.

I stood up straight, raised my left leg, and placed it on the first step. Then, I placed my right boot on the next step.

And that's the way it went, slowly, warily, as we climbed the stairs in total darkness, not able to see anything, not even a single pinprick of light. Angela held my left hand, and I held my right hand straight out, waving it back and forth, feeling my way through the blackness.

Then, I stopped. My hand had touched something hard in front of me. A solid wall of some sort.

"What's the matter?" Angela asked.

"There's something here," I said, and I rapped on the wall with a bare knuckle. The surface was hard and smooth, but it wasn't solid and dense like brick or mortar. My best guess was that it was wood.

"There's a wall or a door here," I said, and I let go of Angela's hand and placed both of my palms on the wall in front of me. I pushed and felt it give just a little bit. Then, I felt around a bit more, searching for a knob, but I didn't find anything.

"Help me push," I said. "This is a wall or a door of some sort. Maybe we can get it open."

Angela took a step up next to me, and we both pushed as hard as we could.

The wall or the door—whatever it was—moved a little bit.

"We're doing it!" I said. "Keep pushing!"

Suddenly, there was a violent, defiant snapping of breaking wood. The wall gave way. Angela and I went tumbling forward, falling down onto our hands and knees. And although we were still in darkness, I knew where we were.

"We made it!" Angela exclaimed. "We're back in the house!"

And we were. We quickly scrambled to our feet and looked around. Our surroundings were black and gloomy, but it wasn't nearly as dark as it had been in the basement. Soon, our eyes adjusted, and we could make out murky images in the room.

"Where are we?" Angela asked.

"Looks like we're in a bedroom," I said.

Carefully, I stepped off the wall we had knocked down. I made my way to a wall where I found a light switch and flicked it up.

The sudden explosion of light was nearly blinding, and I immediately squinted. So did Angela. Actually, it was only a single light that had turned on, in a fixture on the ceiling in the center of the room. But it seemed as bright as the sun, at least for a moment.

After a few seconds, our eyes adjusted to the new light, and I looked around. Angela was still standing where she'd stopped, and now I could see that we'd knocked over a bookcase. There were hardcovers and paperbacks strewn all over the floor.

"Those steps were hidden by that bookcase," I said. "It's a secret passage into the basement."

"But why did the other staircase vanish?" Angela asked, stepping off the fallen bookcase and walking toward me.

I shrugged and shook my head. "I don't know," I replied, "and I don't care. I just want to find my dad and get out of here."

But we couldn't find my dad. We left the bedroom, and I called out to him, shouting and listening, listening and shouting, wandering through the house.

Dad never responded.

"Now what?" Angela said.

We were standing in the living room, next to the contraption Dad had built.

"We're getting out of here," I said, and I picked up my gloves. Angela, too, reached down and picked up her gloves.

"What do you mean?" she asked.

"We're taking the van and going for help," I said.

"You . . . you can drive?" she asked and gave me a puzzled, disbelieving look.

"Well, I've never really done it before," I said. "But I've watched Mom and Dad drive hundreds of times. It's a cinch. You just turn the key, put 'er in gear, and step on the gas. And use the steering wheel, of course."

I could tell Angela was apprehensive, but before she had a chance to speak, I continued.

"Think about it, Ang. What else can we do? Dad is missing, this place is haunted, and we're alone."

"And we're in the middle of a blizzard," Angela said sharply. "I don't think it's the best time for you to try out your driving skills. Skills that you don't even have, anyway."

The wind continued to howl around the house, and in my mind, I saw a giant, white witch, high as the clouds, sweeping her bony hands and arms over us, directing the wind and the snow and the ice and the sleet.

And I was going to learn to drive. I was going to learn to drive, and the white witch was laughing at me.

"Let's go," I said, and it sounded more like an order.

Angela pursed her lips. Her eyes bore into mine. I could tell she didn't like the idea, but I think she also realized that we were out of options. We had to go for help, and the van was our ticket out. Even if we were in the middle of a blizzard, and even if I'd never driven a vehicle before.

And so, with Angela following me, we walked through the living room, down the hall, through the foyer, through the front door, and into the raging blizzard.

16

The key was in the ignition.

For a brief moment, I had been worried that Dad had taken his keys with him. When we're at home or out somewhere, he always locks the van and takes the keys. But other times, if we're somewhere he's sure the van won't get stolen, he'll leave it unlocked and the key in the ignition.

"You sure about this?" Angela said, closing the passenger door as a blast of wind sent a burst of snow into the van. It swirled like confetti for a moment, and then the door was closed and the snow settled. The winter witch snarled and hissed outside, beyond the van, and we were safe inside, away from her prying, chilly fingers.

"Sure, I'm sure," I said. "Now, let's see . . . ."

I reached out and turned the key. Instantly, the engine flared to life. The headlights turned on automatically, illuminating a churning wall of white snow in front of us.

"Put your seat belt on," I said, and Angela did. I put on my belt and then found the automatic button on the side that moved the seat forward. I had to adjust it all the way up, because my legs were much shorter than Dad's. Even so, I could barely touch the gas pedal.

"Ready?" I asked.

"As long as you are," Angela replied.

Using the lever on the steering column, I put the van in reverse, looking in the rearview mirror to make sure I wasn't going to back into something. I turned, stopped, and put the van into drive.

"How can you even see anything?" Angela asked.

"I'll go slow," I said.

I pressed on the gas pedal, and the van inched forward. If the snow slowed us any, I wasn't aware of it. Of course, I'd never driven before, so I had no experience behind the wheel. The only thing I knew was that we were moving forward, and that was a good thing.

Soon, we were inching along the snow-covered driveway. My confidence was growing. On the steering column, I found the windshield wipers and turned them on. They smacked back and forth, back and forth, as we slowly crept down the narrow driveway.

And as we moved, I could feel the tires slipping and sliding. A couple of times, the back end of the van twisted and fishtailed. Angela cringed in the passenger seat, gripping the arm rest with one hand and the console with the other.

"Don't you think you're going a little fast?" she asked nervously.

"I'm not going very fast at all," I replied. "I'm

being careful. When we get to the main road, I'll—"

Without warning, the back of the van slid violently to the left. I spun the steering wheel, but it had no effect.

"Do something!" Angela wailed.

"I'm trying!" I shouted.

"If you don't—"

"—I'm doing everything I can!"

Angela screamed, and I gasped and gripped the steering wheel as the van careened sideways, out of control, heading off the driveway and straight for a clump of trees.

How the van came to a stop before hitting the trees, I'll never know. I had panicked, and I hadn't even tried to step on the brake pedal. It was all too new to me, and when I lost control of the vehicle, all I could do was hang on.

But I think it was the snow that saved us. The van was sliding sideways, and there was so much snow that it must have packed up and under the van, causing it to slow. Just as I thought we were going to slam into the trees, the vehicle lurched to a jerky stop. The only sounds I could hear were Angela's quick, panicky gasps and the wind that gnawed at the exterior of the van.

"I can't believe that just happened!" Angela said. "I thought we were going to hit those trees, for sure!"

"Me, too," I said. "We're lucky to be alive."

And I'm lucky I didn't smash Dad's van to pieces, I thought. He'd ground me until I was out of high school.

But I quickly realized that we now had a new set of problems. Using the lever on the steering column, I put the van in reverse and stepped on the gas. The tires whirred and spun, but the vehicle didn't move. I tried putting it into gear and going forward, but the same thing happened. The tires weren't able to get any traction and simply spun around and around.

"Okay," I said simply. "Now, we're stuck. This van isn't going anywhere."

"Now what?" Angela asked.

I thought for a moment.

"We head back to the house," I said.

"Back to the house?!?!"

I nodded and threw my hands up. "We don't have any other choice, Angela. The main road is still too far away to walk in the deep snow. And we can't stay in the van."

"But at least it's warm here," Angela insisted.

"Only while it's running with the heater on. Sooner or later, we'll run out of gas. And as far as we know, there's no help on the way. If we go back to the house, we'll be out of the storm. We can wait it out. We can wait for someone to come looking for us. Besides: if we go back to the house, maybe we can find Dad's phone. Maybe he left it somewhere. If he did, and we find it, we can call for help."

Angela looked away. She knew I was right; she just didn't like the idea of going back to the house, back to the ghosts and whatever other horrors might be waiting for us.

"Hang on," I said, and I unfastened my seat belt, crawled over the console, and scrambled into the back seat. On the floor was a black and red leather bag: a roadside emergency kit. It had been in the van as long as I could remember, but I didn't think it had ever been opened.

I unzipped the bag and flopped it open. There was an array of tools and gadgets, just about anything and everything you'd need for a roadside emergency. There was a small first aid kit, jumper cables, a flashlight, and a pair of gloves. I snapped up the flashlight and clicked it on, relieved to find that the beam was intensely bright, laser-like. Under the pair of gloves was a foot-long red tube that looked like a stick of dynamite. DANGER was written on the side in bold letters.

"What's that?" Angela asked, peering over the seat.

"An emergency road flare," I said, handing it to her. "Hang on to it in case we need it for something."

Angela inspected the flare for a moment and then rolled it over in her hands.

"How do you use it?" she asked.

"The instructions are printed on the side, I think," I said. Angela examined the flare closer and then tucked it away in her winter coat.

I climbed back over the console, sat in the front seat, and turned off the ignition key. The engine died, but the headlights remained on, illuminating the whipping snow. The lights would shut off by themselves.

"Some day this turned out to be," Angela said.

The wind was blowing so hard that heavy gusts shook the van.

"Come on," I said. I opened the driver's side door, slipped out, and battled the fierce wind and snow as I trudged around the van to the other side. Angela was just getting out, and she closed the passenger door.

I clicked on the flashlight. The snow caused the beam to look like a brilliant white sword. Without another word, we began walking through the raging blizzard, through the deep snow, back to the house.

18

One good thing:

Despite the wind and blowing snow biting at our faces, we didn't have any trouble locating the driveway in the deep snow. That's because all we had to do was follow the van tracks back to the house. I knew that, in a few hours, they would be filled in and covered over by new snow. But at the moment, not only could we see the tire tracks, but we were able to walk in them, which made the going a little easier.

"There's the house, right there," I said,

aiming the flashlight beam ahead of us. "I can see a light on."

In another minute or so, the trees on either side of the driveway thinned, and we entered the large yard where the house sat. Here, without the protection of the trees, the wind was stronger than ever. My cheeks were so cold that they were no longer stung by the pounding of snow and ice. I think my face was numb.

"Hey," Angela said, stopping. She pointed. "The light is on upstairs. That's a room on the third floor. We weren't up there, were we?"

"No," I said. "And we turned off all the lights, anyway, except for the ones in the living room and the foyer."

"Your dad must be up there!" Angela said excitedly. "Maybe that's where he was, all along! Maybe he didn't hear us because he was up on the third floor!"

We stood for a moment, the snow and wind and pellets of ice whipping at us. We stared up through the blizzard. On the third floor, a square of creamy light glowed through the storm.

Downstairs, on the first floor, light streamed out of the windows near the front door. And there was faint light coming from the living room window, too.

But something wasn't right. I didn't know what it was, and I couldn't figure it out. Something just seemed odd, seemed off. The house seemed darker, moodier, and more ominous than it had before.

It's just because it's dark out, I told myself. When we got here earlier, it was during the daytime. Now it's dark, and it looks different.

I was staring directly at the glowing third floor window when a dark silhouette came into view in the room. It was a human figure, and it stood in the middle of the window, as if looking down upon us.

"It's him!" Angela shouted. "It's your dad!" She began waving wildly with both hands.

"He can't see you," I said. "The glare from the light in the room reflecting off the glass inside will be too bright."

"But he must know we're out here," she said.

"He must know we're looking for him!"

Then, another silhouette appeared in the window.

Now, there were two figures looking down at us.

Angela stopped waving.

The winter witch screamed in our ears, clawing at our faces and exposed skin with her frozen fingers.

Two figures in the window.

That shouldn't be.

There shouldn't be anyone else in the house besides Dad.

Unless they're ghosts, I thought.

"Can ghosts make shadows?" Angela shouted over the raging wind.

"I don't know," I said. "But we're going to find out."

"No, we're not," Angela said defiantly. "I changed my mind. We are not going back into that house."

"We don't have any choice, Angela," I said.

"Yes, we have coats and hats and boots and gloves,

102

but with this wind, we won't stay warm for very long. My face is numb already. We'll freeze to death if we stay out here."

"Quinn, I am not going back in that house."

"You'll freeze to death," I repeated. "If you're like me, your cheeks are already frozen. We have to get inside where we can at least get out of the weather and get warm."

This seemed to make sense to her. As much as I wasn't sure about going back inside the old house, we couldn't stay outside. My feet were already starting to get cold.

"Come on," I said. "We'll be okay."

I looked up as we started walking toward the house. In the window on the third floor, the two dark silhouettes had vanished.

19

On the porch, the snow had already covered most of our footprints that we'd made only a short while before. Looking around, it looked like we'd already gotten about ten inches of snow since it had started falling earlier in the day . . . and the storm showed no signs of letting up. The winter witch was still angry, shrieking in the night, casting her dark spell all across the land.

I opened the front door and strode into the

foyer. Angela followed and closed the door behind me, shutting off a blast of wind and snow. I turned off the flashlight.

"Do you think that was your dad upstairs?" Angela asked.

"I don't know," I said. "Right now, I'm likely to believe just about anything. We've already seen ghosts and a vanishing staircase. Speaking of . . . ."

I turned and looked into the closet.

The staircase was gone, the secret passage was no longer there. Only a wall remained.

"But . . . but . . . ." Angela stammered.

"I know," I said. "I can't make sense of it, either."

"Let's find your dad," Angela said with a shudder. "Let's find him and get out of here. I don't ever want to come back to this house again."

"All right," I said. I felt the same as Angela. It was almost funny, when I thought about it. Earlier in the day, I thought my dad was silly and goofy for believing in ghosts. Now, here I was, not only a believer in ghosts, but terrified by a haunted house!

"Let's go up to that room," I said. "That was probably Dad up there."

"But who was that other person?" Angela asked.

"We were in the basement for a while," I said. "Maybe someone else showed up."

"But there isn't any other car parked outside," Angela said, "and no new footprints."

Angela was right, of course. But we still had to go upstairs. We still had to investigate and find out if Dad was up there. The sooner we found him, the sooner we could go home. The sooner we'd be safe.

We strode slowly down the hall, stopping when we reached the living room. It looked the same. To the left, the kitchen was empty. Everything appeared to be just as we'd left it. I even looked for Dad's phone, thinking maybe he'd set it down somewhere, but I didn't see it.

Slowly, we walked across the living room to the stairs. At the foot of the staircase, I stopped, looked up, and listened. The only thing I could hear was the wind outside.

The steps creaked as we made our way up to the second floor. There, we paused for a moment and gazed down the dark hall. I turned on the flashlight and swept the beam through the corridor.

Nothing.

The stairs made a switchback turn, and we continued up to the third floor, which opened up to a long, dark hallway lined with several closed doors. At the bottom of one of the doors, however, was a bar of light.

"There's a light on in that room," I whispered to Angela. "That's the room we saw from outside. The light's still on."

We walked as quietly as we could in our boots, making our way down the hall, toward the closed door, toward the bar of light bleeding from beneath it. When we were directly in front of it, just inches away, we stopped.

Beyond the door, we could hear noises coming from inside the room. I cleared my throat and then spoke.

"Dad?" I said, my voice rising just a little bit.

There was no reply. Just the same faint shuffling and scuffing noises.

"Dad? Are you there?"

Still no reply.

Holding the flashlight in my gloved left hand, I reached out with my right and grasped the doorknob. It was weird: I could actually feel Angela tense up.

I looked at her.

She looked at me.

There was fear in her eyes, and I knew she saw the same in mine.

"Open it," she said quietly. "Let's get this over with. But let me just say that I think we're going to regret this."

And as I turned the knob and slowly pushed the door open, I instantly realized that Angela was right.

20

Now, you might be thinking that it would have been best if we just left. After all, we didn't have to open the door. We could have just left it closed and hustled away.

But no.

See . . . the whole time, I was worried about my dad. What if something had happened to him? What if he was in that room, just beyond the door, and couldn't answer? What if he needed our help?

That's why we couldn't leave, why we couldn't just walk away. We had to know. We had to help him if he was in trouble.

As the door to the room opened, the noises grew louder. When I released the knob, the door continued to swing open, as if it was doing it all by itself.

But there was nothing that could have prepared us for what we were seeing in the room.

Ghostly figures, like the ones we'd seen in the basement, were moving all around, floating just above the wood floor. They moved fluidly through each other and furniture, and this included a bed that was against the far wall. The strange entities moved through it like hands through smoke.

On the wall to the left was a large, wood dresser with a mirror. The dresser contained shelves with various items on them like small picture frames, perfume bottles, things like that. All of these items were shifting back and forth, moving to and fro, bumping into each other, making the scuffing noises we'd heard when the door was still closed.

And like the ghosts we'd seen in the basement, they didn't seem to be paying any attention to us. They just sort of milled around in the room, not looking at us, not looking at each other. They seemed indifferent to the open door, uncaring about the two kids standing there watching them in disbelief.

"Who are these people?" Angela asked.

Slowly, I shook my head. "I have no idea," I whispered back.

"Well, now that we know you're dad's not here," Angela said, "let's get out of here. I'm beginning to think maybe we're better off in the van, after all."

That sounded like a good idea. I had no idea what was happening, and I wanted to be away from the house as soon as possible. It was obvious Dad was gone. We'd done everything we could, we'd looked everywhere for him, and our searches had turned up nothing.

The door opened wider, and I began to notice a strange wind blowing. Which was odd, because we were inside, and there were no doors or windows open. None that I knew of, anyway.

It grew stronger by the second.

"Do you feel that?" I asked Angela.

We both turned. The wind seemed to be coming from behind us.

"Yeah," Angela replied. "Wind. And it's getting stronger."

A brisk gust rushed past, causing the door to bang against the wall of the bedroom.

"Let's go, now!" Angela shrieked, but by then, it was already too late. The next gust of wind hit us with hurricane force, knocking us off our feet and sending us flying into the air, sailing into the bedroom.

21

As soon as we were knocked off our feet and swept into the room, everything went black. The feeling of confusion was overwhelming. I was in the air, tumbling around, without balance. For a moment, it felt as if I was weightless, as if all gravity was gone. It was a horribly disorienting, confusing feeling.

Then, the wind faded, and I was dropped onto the floor. It was just that quick, too. From the time we were standing by the door until the time I realized I was on the floor was only about five seconds. The darkness retreated, giving way to a gray, hazy fog.

"Quinn!" Angela shouted, and I jumped. She was right behind me, and she'd shrieked directly into my ear.

I rolled over onto my hands and knees. Angela was on her side, wide-eyed, mouth open, staring up at me.

"Get up," I said. "Are you okay?"

Angela got to her knees and paused.

"I think so," she said.

We both turned our heads and looked around.

"Are we still in the bedroom?" she asked.

"We must be," I replied, "but it sure doesn't look like it."

All around us, the only thing we could see was a thick, gray fog. It reminded me of a book I'd read about Florida, about terrifying creatures that lived in the fog. That book gave me nightmares for weeks, and every time I saw thick fog, it freaked me out.

That's what it was like in the bedroom. The fog, or whatever it was, was so thick that we couldn't see the walls, the bed, the ceiling, or the dresser. I could barely see Angela, and I could hardly see the floor.

"What . . . what just happened?" Angela asked quietly as she stood.

"Your guess is as good as mine," I replied. I turned my head, and my body followed, slowly, moving all the way around in a complete circle. There was nothing to see, except hazy, gray mist. Most alarming, I didn't see a door. The fog seemed to go on forever and ever.

"Just when I thought things couldn't get any weirder, this happens," Angela said. Her voice trembled. She was scared, and so was I.

But this wasn't anything new. We'd already been scared a number of times since arriving at the house. However, what had just happened seemed darker, more sinister, and more serious. It was bad enough being scared out of our minds in the basement, having the stairs vanish and then those strange ghosts appear. But now it was as if we weren't even in the house anymore, as if we'd somehow been transported through space and time to a different place altogether. It was as if we were marooned on a strange planet, alone in an endless cloud.

But that wasn't right, either. Because we were about to discover that we most definitely were not alone. There was someone else—or something else— here.

"What's that?!?!" Angela hissed, grabbing my arm and nearly jerking it out of my shoulder socket.

A large, dark form was appearing in the fog, slowly coming toward us.

22

Through the fog, it was impossible to see who—or what—was coming toward us. There were no sounds, no footsteps . . . just a dark blob that was growing bigger and bigger.

Angela took a step closer to me. "What is it?" she whispered.

I shook my head slowly, and once again scanned my surroundings, hoping to see some way out, hoping that maybe a door or a path might magically appear. Of course, none did.

"Quinn, is that you?"

The relief that went through my body was electrifying. I'd know that voice anywhere.

"Dad!" I shouted, and I ran toward his dark form. I couldn't actually make out any of his features until I was only a few feet away, but I leapt at him and wrapped my arms around him, giving him a big hug. Angela did, too, and the three of us stood there for a moment, in a solid embrace.

"I can't believe we found you," I said, finally taking a step back. "We've been looking all over for you."

"I've been looking for you guys, too," Dad said.

"Where did you go?" I asked.

Dad shook his head slightly. He looked confused.

"I . . . I don't really know," he replied. "I found a hidden passageway in the foyer closet, and I—"

"We found that, too!" I said, nearly shouting.

"There were steps that went down into the basement—"

"—we went down them," Angela interjected, "but then they disappeared, and we were trapped!"

"I don't know what's going on," Dad said. "In all of the times I've spent hunting ghosts and exploring haunted houses, I've never seen anything like this."

It's pretty scary when your very own dad admits something like that. Grownups are supposed to know everything. Or at least they want us kids to think they know everything.

"So, what do we do now?" I asked.

"Well, there has to be a way out," Dad replied. "There must be some way home."

"This is a nightmare," Angela said. "I can't believe this is happening to us. I feel like I'm going to hear my mom yelling any minute, telling me to get up, that I need to get dressed and ready for school."

"Don't worry," Dad said. "We'll find our way out of here. How did you guys get here?"

"We were looking for you," I replied, and I

told him all about how we'd been in the basement, of the strange ghosts we'd seen. I told him I tried to drive the van to go for help, but got it stuck on the side of the driveway. He wasn't even mad about that.

"We'll worry about the van and the snowstorm later," Dad said. "First, we need to figure out where we are and find a way out. But for the time being, we're together. We're safe."

"Maybe . . . maybe not," Angela said quietly. She raised her arm and pointed. "Look!"

23

Something was coming toward us, and I knew right away that it wasn't a person. And I was pretty sure that it wasn't a ghost, either. Whatever it was, it was tall—very tall—and tube-like, slowing twisting sideways, back and forth, like a giant snake reaching down, like a vacuum cleaner from the sky, sweeping back and forth—

A loud, low rumble began, shaking the floor. Dad grabbed my arm, and then Angela's. There was a roaring sound, like an approaching semi-truck.

"Hang on tight!" he said.

"What is it?!?!" I said, yelling over the growing noise. The rumbling and roaring had intensified, and I had to shout so my voice would be heard.

And if what had happened to us already wasn't unbelievable, what we were seeing was something impossible.

It was a tornado!

The enormous tube-like entity was whirling and spiraling, sweeping the ground in a searching pattern, while the other end of it rose up, reaching into the gray sky, where it vanished.

Already, the wind around us was growing stronger and stronger, jostling us about, whipping at our clothing. I remembered the experience we'd had when that strange wind had sucked Angela and me into the bedroom, and I was sure that I wasn't going to like being carried off by a tornado.

"Get down on the ground!" Dad ordered as he pulled us close. "We can't outrun it! Get down and huddle close! Don't let go of me!"

The three of us fell to our knees and collapsed to the floor, holding each other tightly. By now, the roar was deafening, so loud that it was painful. I wanted to cover my ears with my hands, but that would mean I would have to let go of Angela and Dad. If I did, I was sure that I would be swept away by the powerful, gusting winds of the tornado.

And for a split second, time seemed to stop. For some reason, I suddenly remembered Mrs. Bradshaw, my teacher, giving our class a writing assignment. We were supposed to write a three page story about something unbelievable—but true—that happened to us. I had written a story about how I caught a huge fish with my bare hands while vacationing at a lake. The fish had become stranded in shallow water, effectively trapping it. I had been able to catch it. It was nearly as big as I was! I carried it to deeper water and let it go.

I thought that was a cool story, and pretty unbelievable. But Mom, Dad, and a few other people had been there and watched it happen. Mom was even able to take a picture. She printed the photo, and I attached it to my assignment for proof.

But what was happening to us now was far more incredible, much more unbelievable than catching a big fish with your hands. I knew that even if I wrote down everything that had happened so far, no one would believe me. That is, of course, if I ever had the chance. The way things were going, I didn't know if we were going to make it out of the house alive.

Then, the unthinkable happened. Despite how hard we were holding onto each other, despite how tightly we clung for our lives, the wind tore the three of us from each other, sending us flying and tumbling in different directions. I heard Angela scream, but her voice was quickly drowned out, washed away by the fury of the tornado.

As quickly as the tornado swept me away, it vanished. The sound of the raging wind died off quickly, and I was motionless, hanging in the air like a puppet. I felt no sensation of gravity at all, no way of knowing which was up or down. I could move about freely, but I couldn't go anywhere. At least, it didn't seem like it.

And my surroundings had changed, too. Instead of seeing the endless soup of fog, I could now make out what appeared to be dead trees, their leafless limbs reaching out and up, frozen in death.

Then, a horrible realization came over me.

Is this what it's like? I wondered. Am I . . . am I . . . dead?

No, I don't think I'm dead, I thought. If I was dead, I probably wouldn't be able to move my arms and legs. I held my hands out in front of my face, inspecting my fingers and palms. I looked about as normal as ever.

But, then again, I had never been dead before. I had no idea what it felt like.

Gradually, I became aware of other things in my surroundings. Murky forms and shapes began to appear, and it was then that I realized that not only were they moving, but I was moving, too. I was drifting in this strange realm, moving about by some unseen and unfelt breeze.

"Quinn?"

I turned to look at one of the forms that was drifting toward me.

"Angela?!?! Is that you?"

Dumb question. Of course it was her. I recognized her voice. She was drifting closer to me, on a collision course. Thankfully, we were both moving slowly, and we both reached out our arms to stop each other from colliding. I grabbed hold of her arms just above her elbows, and she gripped my forearms.

The terror in her eyes was unlike anything I had ever seen. Angela isn't one to get scared easily, but what had happened to us, and what was currently happening to us, was something she and I had never experienced before. I'm sure that my face depicted the horror I was feeling as well.

"Quinn! Angela!"

"Dad!" I shouted back. "Where are you? I

can't see you!"

"I'm over here!" Dad replied. "I think I can see you two, and I think I'm moving closer. But there are a lot of other things out here, too."

Dad was right. Hanging in the misty, murky darkness were other entities, and I suspected that they were ghosts. Thankfully, none of them were moving close; none of them seemed to be moving in our direction.

And Dad was drifting closer and closer, but on his current course, he was going to miss us. It was like being an astronaut in outer space. Dad was going to pass by us, just a few inches out of our reach. There was nothing that we could do.

Unless—

"I have an idea," I said. "Quick! When Dad is about to drift by, I'm going to put my boots on your leg and try to push myself out to Dad. With any luck, I'll be able to grab his hand."

"But what if you push me away?" Angela asked.

"You'll need to grab my boots to make sure that doesn't happen. Do it! Now!"

I had run out of time, and I couldn't explain any more. And I wasn't going to simply hang in empty space and watch my dad drift by!

Still holding Angela's arms, I drew my legs up and placed the soles of my boots on Angela's thighs, just above her knees. I pushed, and she let go of my forearms as I launched, reaching out toward Dad, who already had a free hand extended.

"Got you!" Dad exclaimed, and in the same instant, I felt the reassuring grip of Angela's hands on my legs, just above my boots.

"Hang on!" I said to her.

Without much difficulty, the three of us were able to pull ourselves together into a tight knot.

"That was close," Dad said. "That was good thinking, Quinn."

"Are . . . are we dead?" Angela asked.

"I was wondering the same thing," I replied. "But I don't think so."

"I think we're in some parallel world," Dad said. "Scientists have theorized about this for years, but there's never been any proof or evidence."

"What's a parallel world?" Angela asked.

"It's a world that exists in the same space in which our world exists," Dad said, "only in a different time. At least, that's what the theory is."

"It sounds crazy," I said.

"Maybe so," Dad said. "But that's the only explanation I've got. For some reason, this house must be some sort of portal, some sort of doorway into this realm."

Angela looked puzzled. "But how can we exist in the same space in a different time?" she asked. "That doesn't make any sense."

Dad shook his head. "Like I said," he continued, "it's only a theory. None of it's proven."

"The question is," I said, "how do we get out of here, so we can go home?"

As if in response to my question, our attention was drawn to a large, dark form that was drifting toward us. This figure grew in size as it came closer, and if it didn't stop, I was certain that it was going to hit us.

Or worse.

But as it came closer, we could make out the features of a man. His form and features were distorted, and there was very little muscle on his bones. His eyes were gone, and we could see only the black holes of empty sockets. His mouth was open a tiny bit, exposing rotting, broken teeth. His skin—if you could call it that—had mostly wasted away and fallen off. Some of it, though, still remained, like little pieces of crusty, brittle leather.

And when he spoke, the great mystery of what was happening was made clear. The puzzle was about to be solved, our burning questions were about to be answered.

But just because we had answers, it didn't mean we were going to make it out alive . . . .

25

The creature—or whatever it was—spoke.

"You are not welcome here." His voice was weird and raspy, like he'd swallowed a handful of nails and rocks.

For a moment, the three of us said nothing. I was terrified, and I knew Angela was, too. Even my dad seemed frightened, and I think there isn't too much that scares him.

"Well," my dad said. "We're not that thrilled

about being here, either. In fact, I'd kind of like to know where we are."

"You are in the real world," the entity replied in that same, gravelly voice. "This is the only world there is. However, you have entered into a corner of the world where space and time do not exist."

Huh? I thought. How can there be a place where space and time don't exist?

"We'd be happy to be on our way," Dad said, sounding very polite, "if you could be so kind as to show us the way out."

"I will allow you to leave on one condition," the creature said. He drew even closer, and if I could have taken a step back, I would have. But I couldn't.

"You must promise to never return. If you do return, you will never be allowed to leave."

"Perfect," Angela said, and she actually sounded happy. "Sounds like a deal to me. Show us the way out of here."

"But wait!" Dad said. "I need to know more about this place before we go. Who are you?

Where is this place?"

Although the strange entity didn't have any eyes, I could almost feel his gaze or his soul or his thoughts boring into me. I had an eerie suspicion that he might even be able to read my mind, and that made me uneasy.

"The man who built this home," he said, "worked at a funeral home. His job was to prepare the bodies for burial at a cemetery. For this, he was paid very well.

"However, when the cemetery became full, he did not want to purchase more land for another cemetery. So, instead of burying the coffins and caskets, he brought them here, to this house."

A dagger of ice sliced down my spine as I remembered the coffin Angela and I had discovered in the basement.

Dad spoke. "But he still charged people to have their loved ones buried," he said.

The creature nodded slightly. "Yes. He was not a good man, and now that he himself has passed on, he is paying dearly for his . . . indiscretions."

That's when I realized something. I was sure by now that I wasn't dead, but I was as close to death as I'd ever come. In fact, as crazy as it sounded, I knew that the creature in front of us was not among the living. Oh, I'm sure that at one time he was, but not now.

And then, with a growing, ballooning horror, I suspected something else. My suspicion was so strong that I had to ask. I had to know.

"This . . . this guy that you're talking about," I said. "Is . . . is that . . . is that you?"

The question seemed to stun him, and I knew right away that I'd asked the wrong question . . . .

26

I quickly spoke again, backpedaling, trying to explain, trying to take back my words.

"I mean, I'm sorry if—" I started to say, but the hideous creature interrupted.

"Yes, you are correct, I am afraid. But I will explain no further! There are some things you are not to know! Now! Begone, all of you! Do not ever come back!"

Quickly, he made a wide, sweeping motion

with his arm, and in the next instant, the three of us were standing in the living room. I nearly fell, as my body had become used to hanging weightless in the air. Sudden gravity was a shock and a surprise.

"Let's get out of here while we still can!" Angela urged.

"Yeah," I said. "You heard what that ugly dude said. Let's get out of here and never come back!"

Dad looked at his pile of equipment that was in the living room.

"I can come back and get this later," he said. "But I've got to get you two home."

I couldn't believe Dad would even think about returning to the house, but I wasn't going to question it. I wanted out of the house, and I wanted out now.

The three of us hustled to the front door, and Dad threw it open. We were greeted by a blast of frosty wind and a heaping wave of snow.

"How far away is the van?" Dad asked as he stepped out onto the porch and into the snow.

"Not too far," I said. "But it's stuck. It slid off the drive and into a small ditch."

"I might be able to rock it back and forth and get it out," Dad said. "It's all-wheel drive, so we might be able to get unstuck."

"I don't care," Angela said as the three of us began hiking through the snow. "I just want to be somewhere away from that house. Somewhere safe."

The snow and ice tore at my face as we made our way along the driveway. Although it was dark, we could make out the white path of the drive as it wound through the dark trees. Our tracks in the snow, including those of the van, were already filled in by new snow.

"We should be getting close," I said to Dad.

"I think I see it, up ahead," Dad replied. "Did you leave the keys in it? And when did you learn to drive?"

"He didn't," Angela replied. "He faked it. That's why we crashed."

I ignored her comment. "Yeah, I left the keys in the ignition. And Angela's right, sort of. I just did the best I could, trying to remember everything from watching you drive."

"Well, at least you didn't get hurt," Dad said.

I was glad to hear him say that. I thought he was going to be mad because I drove the van and got it stuck. But he was probably just glad that we were okay and that our nightmare was coming to an end.

We found the van easily enough and piled inside. Dad turned the key, and the engine roared to life. I sat in the passenger seat, and Angela sat in the seat behind me.

"Hang on," Dad said.

He began rocking the van back and forth by shifting it from Drive to Reverse over and over. I had tried the same thing, but Dad, of course, had a lot more experience.

Unfortunately, all of Dad's experience wasn't good enough. The van moved, it slipped and slid, but it still wouldn't come out of the ditch. Dad finally got out and looked under the van.

"I can't see because it's so dark," he said. "But it looks like there's a lot of snow packed into the undercarriage. We're going to need a tow truck . . . and I left my phone in the house."

I knew what he was going to say before he spoke.

"You guys hang tight. Keep the doors locked. I'll leave the van running, because I'm only going to be gone a couple of minutes."

But a couple of minutes came and went.

Followed by a couple more.

And more.

Finally, after nearly twenty minutes had gone by, we knew that something was wrong.

We also knew, despite the fact that we didn't want to do it, despite the fact that the creepy old ghost had told us never to go back to the house, we were going to have to go look for Dad. I knew something had happened to him. Maybe he was in trouble, at that very moment.

So, we left the van. Once again, we set out on a search for my dad.

But this time, the consequences were going to be disastrous.

27

"I don't think this day is ever going to end," Angela said as she slipped out of the van and into a burst of snow. I turned off the ignition, and the engine died. I got out and closed the door as I exited.

"Me neither," I said. "But it'll be over soon. I just don't know what happened to Dad."

"I wish there were some other houses around," Angela said. "Somewhere we could go for help. We shouldn't be doing this. We're just kids."

"Well, we didn't plan on any of this happening," I replied. "All I wanted to do was go sledding after we helped Dad set up his ghost hunting equipment. I never thought things were going to turn out this way."

"Well, we'll find your dad and then get out of here," Angela said, sounding hopeful.

I, however, wasn't that optimistic. The only thing I could imagine was that maybe Dad misplaced his phone; maybe it wasn't where he thought it would be, and he was looking for it.

But it wasn't a very convincing thought. Deep down, I knew something had happened to Dad . . . and Angela and I were going to find out.

Through the blowing snow, we saw the dark outline of the house. All of the lights were off.

"That's not good," I said. "Dad wouldn't have turned off all the lights."

"Where's your flashlight?" Angela asked.

"I lost it when we got sucked into that room upstairs," I replied.

We stepped onto the dark porch. The front door was closed, and I turned the knob and pushed

146

it open. Before I went inside, I reached in to flip the light switch.

Nothing happened.

"I think the power's out," I said, flipping the switch a couple of times. Nothing happened.

"What do we do now?" Angela asked.

"Wait here," I replied. "I'll go see if I can find Dad, and I'll come back."

"No way!" Angela said. "You're not leaving me alone! I'm going with you, even if we have to go—"

And that's when we heard Dad, screaming from somewhere inside the house.

28

Without another word, without waiting for Angela, I spun and tore through the foyer. I raced down the dark hall and stopped at the living room. I heard Angela's footsteps coming up behind me.

"Dad!" I shouted. "Dad! Where are you?!?!"

There was noise coming from the gigantic contraption in the living room. Absently, I reached over to flip a light switch. Of course, nothing happened, and I felt like a goof for forgetting the power was out.

"Dad!" I shouted again. "Are you in here?!?!"

I could hear muffled sounds of a struggle coming from the big contraption in the living room, but it was too dark to see anything. Carefully, I waded through the gloom as fast as I could.

A movement at the front of the machine caught my eye.

"Dad?!?!" I shouted.

Suddenly, I realized what I was seeing. Before me in the darkness, protruding from Dad's homemade machine, was a pair of legs! Amazingly, they were extending out from the computer screen!

"What's that?!?!" Angela shrieked.

"That's Dad!" I screamed. "Help me! He's getting sucked into the other world through the computer screen!"

For a split second, I realized how silly that comment sounded . . . but I didn't have time to figure out why things were happening the way they were. All I knew was that Dad was in a lot of trouble.

Although it was dark, I could see the shadowy forms of Dad's legs coming out of the computer screen. But I couldn't see the rest of him! It was the most bizarre scene I've ever witnessed in my life.

"Help me!" I shouted again as I grabbed one of Dad's legs. "Grab a leg and pull!"

I wrapped both arms around one of Dad's legs and pulled with every ounce of strength and energy I had. I could feel Dad struggling, trying to free himself, but he wasn't making any sounds. I knew that, somehow, he was in between the two worlds. And I was sure that if we didn't save him, he'd be pulled into the other realm, and we'd never see him again.

But no matter how hard we pulled, he wouldn't budge. In fact, we lost a little ground, as I could feel him slowly getting pulled farther and farther into the computer screen, into the dark realm.

"I'm pulling as hard as I can, and it's not doing any good!" shrieked Angela.

"Keep trying and don't let go!" I shouted back. "Hang on! Hang on! Hang—"

But our efforts weren't good enough. Whatever was pulling Dad was a lot stronger than we were, and suddenly Dad's legs were gone. He'd been pulled completely into the computer monitor.

Angela and I tumbled to the floor, where we sat for a moment in the darkness, our hearts pounding, our lungs heaving. Outside, all around the old house, the winter witch shrieked louder than ever, howling at the walls and screaming at the windows. I had never felt so alone, so frightened and afraid in my life. I couldn't be more afraid than I was at that very moment—until I realized that something was coming down the stairs . . . .

29

A horrible feeling gripped my entire body. Throughout the day, there had been moments when I'd really been scared—horrified, even—but nothing compared to the feeling that had suddenly come over me. I felt both cold and hot; frozen, yet sweating.

And what made matters worse was that I couldn't move. I've heard people talk about being so scared that they couldn't move, but that never made sense to me. I figured that if you were that frightened, you'd probably be able to move pretty fast, so you could get away from whatever was scaring you.

Now, I knew exactly what it felt like. I was frozen solid, as stiff as a tree trunk, while the monstrous, gruesome horror drifted down the stairs . . . and stopped.

"Oh . . . my . . . oh . . . no," Angela stammered quietly. I was sure that she, like me, was incapable of moving. And once we saw the horrible, hideous thing standing at the foot of the stairs, I knew that escape was going to be impossible.

All of the lights began flashing in the house, surging on and off like lightning bolts. The flashes created after-images in my mind that had a hypnotic effect. The result was that I felt even more mesmerized than ever, unable to move, powerless to even flinch, despite the thin rivers of horror needling through my veins.

And the thing that had stopped at the bottom of the staircase was a monster . . . but it was more than that. Up until then, the strange apparitions we'd seen were smaller and more human-like in appearance. This thing wasn't anything like that at all. Oh, in some ways it was like a human. It had legs, a torso, arms, and a head, but that's where all similarities ended.

"What . . . in . . . the—" Angela stammered again, her voice so low I could barely make out what she was trying to say.

The thing was taller than an average-sized man, but twice as wide. It was covered in both hair and scales, and its eyes were red and flaming. Bubbling drool fell from its open mouth, which held rotten, decaying teeth. Just its mere presence was electrifying . . . and not in a good way.

Without warning, my arm was seized by something. The sudden jolt broke the spell. To my shock and horror, I turned to see an arm jutting out from the computer screen! The screen had seemed to take on a liquid property, as if it were made out of some sort of soft, pliable membrane. You would think that an arm through a computer screen would have shattered the screen, but that wasn't the case.

At first, I tried to pull my arm away in fear and disgust, but then I realized:

It was Dad's arm! He was trying to get out!

"Angela!" I wailed as I grabbed Dad's wrist with my free arm. "It's Dad! Help!"

The hideous creature at the bottom of the stairs spoke, while the lights continued to flash.

"You were warned!" it growled. "You were warned to never come back! Now, you will never escape!"

The lights flashed and blazed, and the effect was maddening. Angela gripped one of Dad's arms with both of her hands, and I grasped the other.

"Pull harder!" I wailed. "Harder!"

Dad's head and shoulders came through the screen, which had split open like plastic wrap. I released my hold of his arm with one hand and looped it around beneath his arm pit.

Dad suddenly came tumbling out, knocking over the big machine as he fell to the floor. Angela and I had to step out of the way, trying to pull Dad in the process. The big contraption crashed to the floor, and the house trembled with a thundering shudder.

Lights continued to flash, and the hideous monster remained at the foot of the stairs. One fat arm pointed at us accusingly. A thick string of drool hung from its chin and then dripped to the floor. It was gross.

"You were warned!" the thing growled. "You were warned to never come back! Now, you will pay the price for returning! Now, you will never leave!"

And that's when the house began falling in on us.

30

I had never been in an earthquake before, so I could only imagine that this was what it felt like. My balance was skewered, the floor shook beneath our feet, and pictures and paintings on the walls crashed to the floor in an explosion of shattering glass. Things fell off shelves in the kitchen, and there was a tremendous racket as pots and pans clanged and banged against the tile.

I helped Dad to his feet. "We've got to get

out of here!" he shouted. "Follow me!"

He climbed over his broken contraption, and I was right behind him. Angela circled around the unit.

The house continued to tremble and shake and rock violently. Pieces of the ceiling—plaster, chunks of wood, things like that—fell all around us. They bounced off my shoulders and head, but most were so small that I hardly noticed them.

A large, wood beam suddenly came crashing down directly in front of Dad, followed by a snowfall of smaller debris that rained upon us. The beam blocked our way out, but only for a moment. Dad scrambled over it and turned around, extending his arms. I grabbed one hand and Angela grabbed the other, and he yanked us so hard he nearly jerked us off our feet, lifting us both up and over the beam.

The house was shaking so violently that it was difficult to walk. Dimly, I was aware of horrible, evil laughter all around, filling the house as it came crashing down around us. More things were falling, and a huge cabinet in the kitchen became unhinged from the wall and crashed to the floor. The large, stainless steel refrigerator fell forward with an enormous clangor. The lights continued to flash like crazed, psychopathic fireworks.

"Follow me!" Dad shouted. He turned and raced down the hall. It was a good thing the three of us were wearing boots, because the floor was covered with sharp shards of broken glass and picture frames. I couldn't imagine what it would have been like if we would have had to make our way down the hall barefoot!

And the only thing I could think of?

Madness.

That's what it was: complete and total madness. The sounds of the house falling in; the crunching glass beneath our feet; and the horrible, wicked laughter that filled our ears was enough to drive a person crazy. In fact, I probably would have gone nuts if I'd had to stay in that house any longer. And for one horrifying, awful moment as Dad reached the front door, I had a terrible thought that it wouldn't open, that it would be stuck, and we would be trapped inside.

But it wasn't. Dad grabbed the doorknob, gave it a quick twist, and threw open the door. It crashed against the wall, its sound becoming lost in the many other sounds of upheaval throughout the house.

Dad leaped forward, tripped on something, and fell headlong onto the porch. I was moving so fast that I couldn't avoid him, and I, too, tumbled out the door, falling on top of Dad before rolling to the side. The front door slammed closed, and for a moment, I didn't move. My heart was pounding, my lungs were heaving. The white witch of winter had shown no signs of leaving, and her cold fingers tore at the exposed skin of my face and ears.

And yet, all was not well. We'd made it out, but our troubles weren't over. I knew this the moment the door slammed, the moment I fell onto Dad, the moment I rolled to the side and lay on my back on the porch, the wind and the snow assailing my face.

True, we had made it out.

But Angela hadn't. She was still inside.

31

I scrambled to my feet and grabbed the doorknob, pushing the door with all my might. Again, I expected it to be locked, to be secure, thinking that I'd have to use all my strength to open it. Thankfully, it opened easily . . . but I couldn't believe the scene unfolding in the foyer and in the hallway.

Angela had her back to me, facing the hallway. The hideous, horrible creature that had been at the foot of the stairs was in the hall, slowly coming toward us.

"Angela!" I shouted. "Come on! Let's go!"

If she heard me, she didn't respond . . . and it was then that I saw what she was holding in her right hand.

The emergency road flare.

I'd forgotten all about it. It had been in our van, and she'd shoved it inside her coat pocket. Now, she held it in her right hand like a weapon.

"I'm getting rid of this thing!" Angela screamed above the sounds of the crumbling house. "Otherwise, I'm going to have nightmares for years!"

"Have you lost your mind?!?!" I shouted. "Leave it alone, and let's just get out of here!"

By now, Dad had climbed to his feet.

"Angela!" he ordered. "Don't! Don't do—"

It was too late. In the next instant, Angela had grasped the flare's cap and snapped it off. Holding the cap with her left hand, she struck it against the tip of the flare, much like striking a match.

Nothing happened.

"Angela!" I wailed.

Angela repeated the procedure, striking the cap against the tip of the flare.

There was a sudden flash and a burst of flame as the flare roared to life, spewing a six-inch dagger of yellow flame. She held it high in a show of triumph, but only for a moment. Then, she drew it back over her right shoulder and, like a major league baseball player, let it fly.

The flare tumbled through the air, cartwheeling down the hall, end over end, tumbling, tumbling—

—and hit the horrible monstrosity square in the middle of its body.

The effect was like a match to a pool of gasoline. There was a discernable whoomp! sound as the flare struck the creature, and in less than a second, it was fully engulfed in an enormous ball of twisting and turning orange and yellow flames. A wall of heat hit us, and Angela threw her arms up to shield her face.

Dad wasn't waiting any longer. He leapt into

the foyer, grabbed Angela by the back of her coat, and yanked her out onto the porch. He continued pulling, dragging her down the snow-covered steps and into the yard. I followed, and the three of us began wading through the deep snow. The wind and ice lashed at our faces. I felt bad for Dad: he wasn't wearing a coat, a hat, or gloves. His only protection were his denim jeans, his shirt, and his boots. I knew he was probably freezing.

But we would be at the van soon. Even if we weren't able to get it unstuck, we could start it and get warm inside. We could get out of the blowing wind and frigid cold.

And maybe most important, we were away from the house. We were away from the nightmare of the creature who threatened to keep us forever. We were cold, but we were safe. Soon, we would be home.

A loud crash behind us caused the three of us to stop. We turned, and I squinted as the snow and ice pellets assailed my eyes. But even from a distance, I could feel a faint heat on my exposed skin.

The entire house was in flames. Yellow and orange tongues were licking into the sky, sending little, glowing satellites spiraling up into the darkness, whipped and whirled by the angry wind. The flames seemed to be alive, tormented and thrashed by the blizzard, fanned to a frenzy by the angry, winter witch.

Holy cow, I thought. We burned down the house. We burned the house down, and we're going to be in a ton of trouble.

But at least, I thought again, at least the three of us are alive. Whatever happens from here on out, at least we're safe. We're safe, and we're alive.

Somehow, that seemed pretty amazing in itself. Yet, that's not where this story ends. Yes, we made it out safe. Yes, we made it out alive. But perhaps the strangest thing of all was yet to happen, when we were at home, the following morning.

When the police showed up at our house.

32

When I awoke the next morning, I was surprised to find that it was after nine o'clock. I never slept in that late, not even on the weekends.

Then, I suddenly remembered everything that had happened the day before, right up to the point where Dad had been able to get the van unstuck from the driveway. I remembered the snow in the headlights as he drove the van cautiously to the main road, and then—

Then, I didn't remember anything after that. I must have fallen asleep in the van.

I rolled out of bed, found my slippers, and walked to the window. I pulled back the drapes.

The snow had stopped, and the sky was gray. There was probably fifteen or sixteen inches of new snow on the ground, dumped by the storm. The winter witch had moved on, spilling her cauldron of white potion all over Grand Haven.

But the next thing I noticed was the dark blue Michigan State Police Suburban parked in our driveway.

"Oh, man," I whispered. "They're coming for us. We're going to get arrested for burning down the house. We're going to be taken to jail."

I began to tremble. I didn't want to get arrested, I didn't want to go to jail. Sure, it had been Angela who had lit the flare. She had thrown it at that creature or ghost or whatever it was. She was the one who'd actually started the fire that burned down the house.

But she might have saved our lives, too. There's no telling what that thing might have done if Angela hadn't done what she did. It had been incredibly brave. Destructive, yes. But necessary. Necessary, and courageous.

And the more I thought about it, I realized that I probably wouldn't be taken to jail. Kids my age don't go to jail. Angela and I probably wouldn't get arrested.

However, Dad might. Dad might get arrested, and he might go to jail. You can't burn down a house and think you're not going to get into trouble.

I spun, raced across my room to my bedroom door, threw it open, and sprinted down the hall. My brother Alex was in the kitchen, eating a bowl of cereal and reading a comic book at the table. He glanced up at me for a second and then went back to reading.

In the living room, Mom and Dad were just saying good-bye to two State Troopers, a man and woman, in dark blue uniforms. Mom was closing the door as I stopped, already out of breath and gasping from the frantic run from my room.

Dad must've seen the panicked look on my

face. He raised his hands, displaying his palms, and began to explain.

"Everything's okay," he said. "I told the police everything that happened, from the time we arrived at the house until the time we left."

"And they're not going to arrest us for burning down the house?" I asked.

Dad and Mom looked at each other.

"No," Dad said, shaking his head. "They aren't going to arrest me. Or you, or Angela."

"But we lit the house on fire!" I said. "And did you tell them about the ghosts? About the crazy things that happened?"

Dad nodded. "I told them everything," he repeated. "I told them the truth." He looked at Mom. Deep concern was written upon both of their faces.

"Then . . . what's wrong?" I asked.

Dad sighed. "Well, there's one thing they're having a hard time believing," he said. "Several things, actually. In fact, I'm having a hard time believing it, too."

"Is it the ghosts?" I asked.

"No," Dad said, shaking his head. "It's the house. You see, when we got home last night, you'd fallen asleep in the van. I carried you to your bedroom. Then, your mother called Angela's parents. I drove her to her house and then came home. I called the police and told them what had happened. They called back an hour later, saying that when the fire department had been to the home, they had found the structure intact."

I was confused. "What do you mean, 'intact?'" I replied. "What does that mean?"

"It means it was fine," Dad said. "It hadn't burned down. In fact, there was no evidence of us even having been there."

Slowly, my jaw slackened and fell. My mouth hung open in dumbfounded amazement.

"But . . . but we . . . we saw it!" I stammered. "All three of us did! You saw it, too!"

Dad shook his head. "I know, I know," he said. "It doesn't make any sense. The police wanted to talk more about it, so they came here to speak to me in person."

I stood there, my jaw hanging open, not

knowing what else to say. My thoughts were spinning, and there were so many of them that my brain couldn't seem to latch on to any single one. Questions came at me and fled just as fast.

"Are you all right?" Mom asked, placing a hand on my shoulder. Her words brought me out of my daze, and I shifted my gaze to her.

"Yeah," I replied with a slow nod. "I just can't believe it. I can't believe it didn't happen."

"Oh, it happened, all right," Dad said. "But what is it that exactly happened? I don't know. We may never know."

Later that morning, I called Angela to tell her about the police and what had happened.

"I know," she said. "They just left."

"They were there?!?!" I exclaimed.

"Yup," she said. "They asked me everything about what had happened last night."

"What did you tell them?"

"I told them the truth," Angela replied. "I told them about the flare and everything. They told me the house didn't burn down. It's crazy. Quinn . . . what really happened yesterday? I mean . . . did all of that happen, or did we just dream it?"

"It was no dream," I said, shaking my head. "It really happened."

School, of course, had been canceled for the day. That afternoon, Angela and I dragged our sleds to a nearby park where there was a big hill, so we could take advantage of the newly-fallen snow. There were about twenty other kids there, sledding down the hill, hiking back up, and sledding down again. When we got tired, we sat down next to a big tree. Thanks to our snowsuits, hats, gloves, and boots, we were as warm and comfortable as we could be.

Except for one thing.

The memory of yesterday. That made me really uncomfortable.

"I just don't understand," I said to Angela. "There are so many things that we don't know. I started making a list of unanswered questions in my head, and I've lost track. There are just too many questions."

"I don't suppose they'll ever be answered,"

Angela said. "I'm never going back to that house ever again."

"My dad said he called the owner of the house this morning," I said. "He wanted to know more about the original owner of the house, a long time ago. But Dad said the number was disconnected, and he can't find anything more about him. It's like the owners don't even exist."

"But that's impossible!"Angela said. "I can't believe that we—"

Angela stopped speaking. Something behind me had caught her attention, and she looked over my shoulder. Her eyes flew open wide, and she pointed.

"Look out!" she screamed.

33

Alarmed by Angela's warning, I turned my head.

A large sled, carrying a kid in a black snowsuit, was barreling directly at us!

I rolled to one side, and Angela rolled to the other. However, the kid on the sled also rolled, tumbling off his sled and into the snow. The plastic sled went flying by us harmlessly, hitting the tree with a loud bonk! and coming to rest upside down in the snow.

In the tumble, the kid's hat went flying, and a gallon of black hair spilled out. That's when I realized that it wasn't a 'him,' it was a 'her.' Powdery snow frosted her black hair and face.

"Sorry 'bout that," the girl said, wiping the snow away from her face. She was grinning. "I got going too fast and lost control."

"Yeah, I guess," Angela snapped. She wasn't too happy about nearly being run over.

"We're fine," I said.

The girl's name was Brittany, and she was from Sault Ste. Marie, in Michigan's Upper Peninsula. She was visiting some relatives and was supposed to have gone home the day before, but the snowstorm caused her family to stay another couple of days, at least until the roads were cleared and travel was safer.

"Yesterday," she said, "our car slid off the road, and we nearly hit some trees. We were really lucky that no one was hurt."

I looked at Angela, and she looked back at me.

"I think we were luckier than you were," I

said.

"Yeah," Angela replied. "What happened to us yesterday was pretty scary."

We told Brittany all about the haunted house, how we'd spent the day there, and all of the things that had happened. She listened with complete fascination, not saying a word.

"So," I said, "that's what really happened yesterday. Do you believe it?"

Brittany shrugged. "It sounds scary," she said. "But I've heard of crazier things happening. In fact, I had something happen to me last year that was just as scary. Maybe worse."

"Really?" Angela said.

Brittany nodded. "That's right," she said. "Come on. Grab your sleds, and I'll tell you all about it while we hike back up to the top of the hill."

And so, while the three of us pulled our sleds through the deep snow, while other kids hollered and shrieked as they whizzed down the hill on their sleds, Brittany told us all about the sea monsters of Sault Ste. Marie . . . .

Next:

Johnathan Rand's
MICHIGAN
CHILLERS®

#18: Sault Ste. Marie Sea Monsters

Continue on for a FREE preview!

Next:

MICHIGAN CHILLERS

#16: Sault Ste. Marie
Sea Monsters

Continue on for
a FREE preview!

It was the perfect summer day, and I mean absolutely, one-hundred percent perfect. The sun was shining, there were only a few breaths of feathery clouds in the sky, the temperature was near eighty.

And me and my new best friend, Zach Kuschman, were at Sherman Park with dozens of other people doing the same thing we were: soaking up the sun, relaxing on oversized, colorful towels, and taking a dip into the cool, rich waters of Lake Superior when the heat became too much to take.

"Man, I need to get a drink of water," Zach said. He rolled to his knees on the beach towel and stood, momentarily blocking the sun and covering me with a deliciously cool shadow. "Want me to bring you back something?"

"I'll take a vanilla ice cream cone with two scoops, fudge and candy sprinkles on top," I said with a smile.

Zach smirked. "Sorry," he said. "Best I can do is bring you a water or a lemonade. I think that's all my mom packed in the cooler."

"I'll take a lemonade if you have an extra," I said.

Zach thrust out his thumb. "Be right back," he said.

"I'll be here," I replied, and his shadow fell away from me. Once again, the hot sun baked my skin, and I gave my arms, legs, and stomach a quick glance to make sure I wasn't getting burned. I'd put more sunscreen on after my last swim, but

I didn't want to take any chances.

If only my friends could see me now, I thought, here beneath the hot sun, over a thousand miles from where they were right now.

It's kind of funny: when I told my friends in Texas—that's where we used to live—that my family was moving to Michigan, they freaked out.

"Michigan?!?!" they said. "Isn't Michigan like the snow capital of the world?" All my friends warned me that I was going to freeze to death.

Of course, Michigan does get a lot of snow, especially where we live in Sault Sainte Marie, or 'The Soo,' as it's often called. It's a small city that borders Canada in what's called Michigan's Upper Peninsula. Sault Sainte Marie in French means 'The Rapids of St. Mary,' and the only thing separating the two countries is the St. Mary's River. And the International Bridge, of course, where thousands of cars and trucks travel between the two countries every day. In fact, The Soo is actually two cities. There is Sault Sainte Marie, Michigan, and Sault Sainte Marie, Canada. It's kind of cool knowing that we can get in the car and drive to another country in just a few minutes, simply by crossing a bridge.

And although the word is actually 'Sainte,' it's hardly ever spelled that way. It's always abbreviated. So, whenever you see it on a map or anywhere, you'll almost always see it as 'Sault Ste. Marie.'

Something else that Sault Ste. Marie is famous for is what's known as the Soo Locks. It's a system in the St. Mary's river that is used to 'lock' big freighters in a confined space, and lower or raise the water level so the ship can pass through. Of course, it's a lot more technical than that, but that's how it was explained to me by my mom when I asked her about it. Lots of people come from all over to see giant freighters pass through, and it's pretty cool. I took some pictures of the lock system and sent them to my friends in Texas.

But what my friends didn't know was that while Michigan does get a lot of snow, the summers are spectacular. It gets hot, too. Not quite as hot as Texas. But in Michigan, there's water just about everywhere. Lakes, creeks, ponds, streams . . . you name it. Beaches and places to swim are all over the place. That's something Texas doesn't have a lot of, except for the coastal areas in the southern part of the state. I think my friends in Texas would like Michigan in the summer, but I don't think they'd care for the winters too much. They were right about that: Michigan winters can be extremely cold, and there's always a ton of snow.

But right now, it was summer. It was summer, I was on the beach at Sherman Park with my best friend, and the day was sunny and hot. Everything about the afternoon was absolutely perfect . . . until a man wading in the water near shore began screaming.

The man's screaming made everyone turn their heads. The beach was crowded, too, with lots of people in the sand and a bunch of people in the water. But when the man began wailing, everyone seemed to stop and stare in his direction, including me.

Not far from shore in knee-deep water, a man about my dad's age, wearing bright red swim trunks, was balancing on one leg. He held his other foot in both hands, and even from a distance, I could see why he was screaming: his leg and foot were covered in blood.

What I didn't see was Zach returning with two cans of lemonade.

"Is that blood on that dude's foot out there?" Zach asked as he sat on the blanket.

"I think so," I said, taking one of the cans of lemonade in my hand. "I wonder what happened."

We stared at the man in the water, holding his foot just above the small waves. He lost his balance once and had to drop his injured leg into the water, and then he limped toward the shore where several people rushed to help him.

"Maybe he was attacked by a shark," Zach said with a chuckle.

"There aren't any sharks in Lake Superior," I said, rolling my eyes. "And there aren't any in the other Great Lakes, either."

"Hey," Zach said, taking a sip of his lemonade. "You never know. There was that kid a few years back that found a real megalodon tooth on the shore of Lake Huron. In fact, that one guy wrote a book about a freshwater megaladon that lived in a lake in Mississippi."

"I read that book," I said. "That guy who wrote it just made it up in his head. He wrote a bunch of books like that. It's just his weird imagination."

"Maybe so," Zach said. "But that book made me think twice before I got in the water again."

The injured man had reached the beach, and a woman was helping him walk. I could hear chattering, but because we were so far away I could only make out pieces of words and sentence fragments like 'sharp rock,' 'bad cut,' and 'stitches.'

"Looks like he's going to be okay," I said. "Sounds like he cut his foot on a rock."

"Good thing he's out of the water," Zach said. "All that blood is bound to attract sharks."

I smiled and leaned back onto the towel. That's one of the reasons I liked Zach so much: he's got a great sense of humor. He's not sarcastic or mean or anything; not like that at all. He just has a funny way of looking at things, and he makes me laugh. I was glad to have him as a friend because of that. But I was also glad to have him as a friend for other reasons . . . because the terror we were about to experience wasn't something anyone would want to go through alone.

We moved from Texas to Michigan in the fall of last year, when my dad got a job at a new factory in Sault Ste. Marie. He's a chemical engineer, and while I don't know a lot about what he does, I know he's pretty smart. But not as smart as Mom. Dad is always losing things around the house and he can never find them. Mom knows where everything is, always. It's like she's psychic or something.

And I have a little sister, too. Bella is only two years old, but I adore her. She's fun to play around with, and she has the cutest, goofiest smile you've ever seen.

We also have a cat. She showed up on our doorstep a few days after we moved to our new home in Michigan. We couldn't find who she belonged to, so we decided to keep her. She pretty much keeps to herself, but she's playful when she wants to be. We named her Dora, and she and Bella are best pals.

I met Zach on the same day we moved in. He was riding past on his bike and saw Mom, Dad, and me carrying things into the house. Bella was playing in the yard with a doll. Zach stopped and asked Dad if we needed help. Dad thought that was pretty cool, and I did, too. Zach helped all day, until the last box was carried inside from the truck. We've been best friends ever since.

"You know," Zach said as we watched the man being helped across the beach by a couple people, "I was only kidding about sharks."

I smirked. "I know that," I said.

"But last week, there were some reports of some sort of strange fish or creature or monster in the St. Mary's River. You know: the river that runs through the city."

I rolled to my side, raising my arm to shield my eyes from the sun so I could see Zach better.

"What sort of monster?" I asked with a grin, knowing that he was going to come up with some crazy story.

"You didn't hear about it?" Zach asked.

I shook my head, still smiling, still waiting for the punchline of the joke. "Nope," I replied.

"I know it sounds weird," Zach said. "But a few people said they saw something strange in the water. There was even a reporter from the newspaper who saw it, and he did a story about it."

"What did he see?" I asked.

Zach shrugged. "He wasn't sure himself. He said it was like a huge shadow beneath the surface of the river. It made a large wake. Whatever it was, he said it was too big to be a normal fish. He was pretty freaked out by it."

"Maybe it was the Soo Locks Monster," I said with a smile. "You know . . . sort of like the Loch Ness Monster, only living here, in the waters between the United States and Canada."

"That would be cool," Zach said, and he gazed out over the clear blue waters of Lake Superior, and the dark band of land mass several miles to the north that was Canada. "Think about it," he continued. A real sea monster, living here, in the lake, or in the St. Mary's River."

"No," I said, rolling to a sitting position and scanning the waters. "I don't think it would be cool at all. I think it would be horrifying."

"Well," Zach said as he fell back onto the towel. "I don't think we have anything to worry about. You know how people tend to make things up. I don't think there is such a monster. But Lake Superior is pretty deep. You never know what might be lurking down there, just waiting for a chance to gobble someone up."

Of course, I didn't believe it, either. Sea monsters aren't real.

But I was wrong. I was wrong, and my first summer in Sault Ste. Marie, Michigan, was about to become a living nightmare.

A few days went by. The weather became kind of pukey, and the temperature fell. It rained on and off, too, and the sky was gray and dull. I talked to Zach on the phone, but we didn't get together. Zach lived close to Sherman Park, but my family lived a couple of miles east, closer to the city and closer to where my dad worked.

But one day Zach sent me a text, wanting me to call him right away. Of course, if it was something important, I don't know why he didn't call me in the first place.

I punched his name in my phone's contact list. I heard it ring once, then Zach's gritty voice squawked in my ear.

"Britt! Are you ready for this?!?!"

I pulled the phone away and winced, surprised by the loudness and excitement of his voice. I smiled and laughed.

"Ready for what?" I replied.

"My uncle has two new kayaks! He left them for us to use if we want, while he goes on a business trip! Wanna go?"

"Yeah!" I said. But then, I thought about it. "I've never been in a kayak before," I said.

"They're a cinch," Zach said. "Really easy. These are the kind you can sit or kneel in. We can take them out to the beach and cruise around in the water. It'll be cool!"

"When?" I asked.

"As soon as it gets warm again," Zach said. "My mom says tomorrow is supposed to be a nice day. How about you meet me over here at my house at ten tomorrow morning?"

"Perfect!" I said.

I ended the call, excited about learning how to kayak, excited about exploring the deeper water beyond the beach, excited about another adventure. I'll admit I was a little fearful of the kayak, but that was only because I'd never been in one before. I'd heard it was easy to tip over in a kayak. However, Zach said I'd learn fast, and I believed him. So my fear about kayaking was quickly erased by my excitement and enthusiasm of learning something new and different.

I went to bed that night, wondering what it was going to be like, wondering how fun it would be. I was so focused on kayaking with Zach that I'd forgotten all about the mysterious sightings of the underwater creature a few weeks before. The entire conversation with Zach had completely slipped my mind, as if it had been erased, as if it had never occurred. I'd failed to remember anything about the strange creature in the water.

Not for long. And if I didn't believe that sea monsters existed in the depths of Lake Superior, stalking the waters around Sault Ste. Marie, well, I was about to learn a lesson I wouldn't soon forget. That is, of course, if Zach and I survived what would be the deadliest experience of our lives.

ABOUT THE AUTHOR

Johnathan Rand has authored more than 90 books since the year 2000, with well over 5 million copies in print. His series include the incredibly popular **AMERICAN CHILLERS, MICHIGAN CHILLERS, FREDDIE FERNORTNER, FEARLESS FIRST GRADER,** and **THE ADVENTURE CLUB.** He's also co-authored a novel for teens (with Christopher Knight) entitled PANDEMIA. When not traveling, Rand lives in northern Michigan with his wife and three dogs. He is also the only author in the world to have a store that sells only his works: **CHILLERMANIA** is located in Indian River, Michigan and is open year round. Johnathan Rand is not always at the store, but he has been known to drop by frequently. Find out more at:

www.americanchillers.com

Join the official

AMERICAN
CHILLERS

FAN CLUB!

Visit www.americanchillers.com for details!

VISIT CHILLERMANIA!

WORLD HEADQUARTERS FOR BOOKS BY JOHNATHAN RAND!

CHILLERMANIA!

**I-75 Exit 313
then south
1 mile!**

Visit the HOME for books by Johnathan Rand! Featuring books, hats, shirts, bookmarks and other cool stuff not available anywhere else in the world! Plus, watch the American Chillers website for news of special events and signings at *CHILLERMANIA!* with author Johnathan Rand! Located in northern lower Michigan, on I-75! Take exit 313 . . . then south 1 mile! For more info, call (231) 238-0338. And be afraid! Be veeeery afraaaaaaiiiid . . . .

All AudioCraft books are proudly printed, bound, and manufactured in the United States of America, utilizing American resources, labor, and materials.

USA